When
Leaves
Fall

A Spiritual Novel

ANDRES PELENUR

To Marieke Van Rosmalen

You were only seventeen when God called you back home,
yet your light burns forever in my heart.

So make your way through this brief moment of time as one who is obedient to nature, and accept your end with a cheerful heart, just as an olive might ripen and fall, blessing the earth that bore it and grateful to the tree that gave it growth.

— MARCUS AURELIUS

Published by Raina Books

910-2345 Yonge St., Toronto, Ontario M4P 2E5

Cover design: Kerry Hynds, Aero Gallerie

Editor: Martha Hayes, Dedicated Editing Services, Raleigh, NC

Proofreader: Julie MacKenzie, Free Range Editorial, Jacksonville, FL

Quote from Meditations, by Marcus Aurelius, translated by Robin Hard (Oxford, UK: Oxford University Press, 2011).

First published in 2018

Printed in the United States of America

ISBN: 9781986829038

PROLOGUE

*T*he silver nameplate on my office door read Dr. L. B. McDermott. But to those who knew me best, I was simply Laura. In the prime of my career, at age thirty-eight, I was diagnosed with cancer. That terrible scourge, melanoma, cast its long, dark shadow over me. Yet the details of my struggle are of minor importance, no more deserving of attention than the sufferings of the patient in the next bed. What mattered most, however, were the extraordinary events that unfolded between treatments when I happened one afternoon to wander into a small stone church whose spire I had noticed from my hospital room window.

I have to admit, I didn't walk into that church to find Jesus. In fact, I had transformed into a proud atheist over the years. Although I was raised Catholic, I saw myself as a woman who had little time for religious nonsense. By the time I made it to medical school, there wasn't any room left in my mind for anything that couldn't be proven in a lab.

Yet something that afternoon pulled me through those tall wooden doors. A faint intuition, a gut feeling perhaps, that within those walls something or someone was waiting for me. I was right. His name was Father Manann.

Over the next nineteen months, I sat in the quiet space of his confessional. For the longest time, all I saw of him were hints of his face through the crisscrossed lattice that divided us. A streak of black hair pressed against a pale forehead and a flash of green-gray eyes. I listened to his whispering voice for hours as it floated through the shadows, sometimes comforting me and, at other times, provoking me. Yet it was only near the end that I was able to grasp the true purpose behind his teachings. They were not only meant to give me solace but to prepare me to receive life's greatest revelation.

ELAINE

I've always been a little ashamed to admit that my marriage to Jeremy Holt was the product of an office romance, but that's what happens when you spend every waking hour at work. I was young, twenty-three to be exact, and it didn't take long for me to become pregnant. On June 3, 1996, my daughter, Elaine, was born. Only three years later, she died of leukemia.

Elaine was born with a healthy wisp of blond hair and the most adorable dimples I had ever seen. A good sleeper from the start, I loved watching her tummy rise and fall while my fingers danced over the pink birthmark above her belly button. She developed like any other healthy child: laughing, sleeping, eating, and keeping us busy with what felt like endless diaper changes. When I held her in my arms, I truly believed the world was a perfect place.

Before we even had time to blink, she moved from struggling to flip onto her stomach to crawling across the carpet. I'll never forget the joy we felt when we first saw her pull herself up to a standing position, holding on to the sofa for dear life. For such a simple moment to have filled us with so much

wonder sounds almost laughable, but it allowed me to understand the depth of love parents have for their child.

We noticed something was wrong when Elaine was just shy of
turning two. She grew more fatigued than normal, her face pale
and drawn. While before she cried for her pureed fruit, we now
struggled to get her to eat past the third spoonful. One afternoon,
while dragging around her favorite stuffed rabbit, she looked up
at me and smiled. Her teeth were tinged red as if she'd just bitten
into a beet. I rinsed her mouth, but her gums ran red again.

I drove to the hospital barely keeping my eyes on the road.
After Elaine's examination, the attending physician handed me
a glass of water to calm me down while we waited for Jeremy
to arrive.

"How's Elaine?" he said, bursting through the door.

"She's fine now," said the doctor. "But we're going to have
to run further tests."

"What kind of tests?" I asked.

The doctor frowned. "I'm sorry, but we need to test for
leukemia."

When I heard the word leukemia, I felt my legs go numb.

Elaine underwent a bone marrow aspiration a few hours
later. The sight of such a long needle piercing into her little hip
was too much to bear, so I bit my thumb to stop myself from
screaming. How could this be happening to my baby girl? I
cried. But the procedure only marked the beginning of
my tears.

The diagnosis of acute lymphoblastic leukemia confirmed
our worst fears. A devastating four-week course of chemotherapy followed. There are no words to describe the pain of
seeing your innocent child, who is not even mature enough to
understand what is going on, suffer so terribly. To see her wince
in pain as the medicine dripped into her arm made me weep
until my eyes ran dry. Even though I didn't believe in God, I

conjured him up in my mind for the sole purpose of cursing him.

More chemotherapy followed, along with further tests to determine if her cancer had been contained. We were hopeful, because leukemia is not as deadly as one might think. In fact, almost eighty percent of patients remain cancer free for five years after their initial treatment. If they pass that milestone, many are cured for life. But Elaine would not be so lucky.

Six months later, her cancer returned. This time, they found it in her lungs and spinal cord. After another round of chemotherapy, they focused a radiation beam into her small head in an effort to stop the cancer from moving into her brain. Those were the worst days of my life.

Watching Elaine, her body thin and frail, lying quietly on my chest as if resigned to her fate, shattered my heart into a million screaming pieces. But instead of giving up hope, something deep inside me rose up in anger. We scrambled to find a matching stem cell donor. When none materialized, Jeremy insisted, against my better judgment, on looking at alternative therapies. Chinese medicines, all kinds of untested supplements, anything that offered hope.

"We need to get to New Mexico," he insisted at one point, referring to a private clinic that promised to reverse cancer through controlled fasts and herbal infusions.

"Over my dead body," I replied.

We fought hard over these decisions.

During our darkest days, we received enormous support from the small army of doctors and nurses who did everything possible to save Elaine. They were an inspiration I'll never forget. My parents, my rock, were always by our side, even though it was as hard on them as it was on us.

After a particularly bad night, Jeremy's mind spiraled into a frenzy.

"She's going to die," he yelled, "unless we try something different."

"Actually, chemo is the only thing that can save her."

"Chemo is what's going to kill her," he snapped back.

After pacing up and down the hospital's hallway, he sat down beside me. "Please," he begged, "let's try something different."

But I refused to budge. No matter how desperate he became, I would not take Elaine off her standard treatment. I simply was not willing to play roulette with my daughter's life.

When Jeremy got it into his head to fly Elaine to some obscure homeopathic clinic in Germany, I put my foot down. By now she was in so much pain, she couldn't even sit up on her own.

"I'm putting her on the next flight to Hannover."

"Shut your goddam mouth," I said.

He punched a hole in the kitchen door while I smashed a ceramic bowl on the floor. All of the disappointments, stress, fear, and hope for a miracle that never arrived left us raw and exhausted.

Less than a week later, she died in my arms.

THE WEDDING CAR

*I*n the early 1960s, my parents moved to America like many an Irish family before them in search for a better life. They had followed the lead of a distant cousin who had settled in Portland, Maine, and, despite the harsh winters, I felt lucky to call that beautiful place home.

My father was a small businessman, an optometrist, and my mother was a part-time ballet instructor. Each time they walked into the room, they struck me as an odd couple. He was short and balding, with a sharp nose and lines down his mouth that made him look perpetually angry, while she was tall and lean, with soft blue eyes and a high forehead. Yet despite the contrast, there was never a doubt they were meant for each other.

After spending all day staring into his patient's eyeballs, my father came home, ate his supper, and retreated into the pages of a book on history or politics. He kept the news channel running in the background, often lifting his gaze to address any politician who came on-screen, to the point where my mother joked that he had missed his calling. Instead of becoming an eye doctor, he should have run for office. At least then he would have put his rhetoric to good use.

Even though I had a natural interest in science and math, my father's passion for politics rubbed off on me. When I graduated from college, I jumped at the opportunity to join Angus King's 1994 campaign for Governor for the State of Maine, joining his office as an Assistant to the Policy Director. It was there where I met my first husband, Jeremy, or the hopeless dreamer as I used to call him.

Jeremy was tall, with curly brown hair and a natural smile that lit up the room. But it was the glint of mischief in his eyes that really caught my attention. Although he was smart, he never used his intelligence to further his own ends. Instead, he devoted his talent to figuring out how to make the world a better place. His interests ranged from setting up a hot-meal program for inner-city schoolchildren to a charity that installed water pumps in African villages, all of which made him quite attractive to me.

We worked into the small hours of the night during the run-up to the election, sometimes agreeing, often arguing, until we became inseparable. After the Governor's victory march, I was promoted to the position of Assistant to the Chief of Staff. Soon after, Jeremy and I married on a golf course overlooking the sea. As our wedding car pulled away, I remember thinking that life couldn't get any better.

YALE

$\mathcal{W}$e were never the same after Elaine's death. We joined a parental support group, but it gave us little solace. We argued and fought on a regular basis over things which would have never mattered before. It was as if my feet were stuck in the mud and I couldn't move an inch. My mother, with typical Irish stubbornness, tried hard to convince me to go to church. But I refused. The mere thought of it filled me with contempt.

Throughout our ordeal, the Governor's office had been supportive, giving me as much time off as I needed. For that I was grateful, but no amount of kindness was able to stop me from falling into a deep depression. Even though I waited for time to heal me, healing never came.

Day after day, I replayed in my mind the details of Elaine's treatments. What we had tried, what we had avoided, and the limits of medical science. I agonized over what else could have been done. One night, while I was staring at the ceiling, unable to fall asleep, I made a monumental decision. I would go to medical school to become a doctor. I vowed then and there to become an expert in pediatric blood cancers. I would dedicate all of my energy to find a cure for leukemia in Elaine's memory. It would serve as my new purpose in life.

Of course, Jeremy hated the idea. He said I was reacting to my depression and that I was too old to start medical school. He reminded me of all the good work we had done at the Governor's office, and how much more there was left to accomplish, but I had lost interest in trying to better the world through politics. I took the Medical College Admission Test, acing it on my first try. I gathered letters of recommendation, one from Governor King himself, and applied to the best schools in the country. When Yale's School of Medicine called me with an offer of admission, I remembered what joy felt like. A few days later, their letter arrived in the mail. When I handed it to Jeremy and saw the look on his face, I knew our marriage was over.

"Don't do this," he begged. "I know you're heartbroken, but running off to medical school isn't going to bring her back."

I hugged him and wept. "I have to do something, so I know she didn't die in vain."

"It doesn't have to be this way."

"How, then?" I asked.

"But what about us?"

I held Jeremy's face in my hands and shook my head. Without Elaine we are nothing, I wanted to say. Yet however hard I tried, the words stayed stuck in my throat.

A FRANTIC CALL

$\mathcal{I}$ counted the days to move to New Haven in the hopes of escaping the sadness that followed me like a shadow. As soon as school started, I threw myself into my studies. Since I was the oldest student in my class, I found it easy to keep to myself. And since I didn't have any interest in socializing, there was little to distract me. Though I can't say my attitude earned me many friends, it did have an upside—I excelled at most of my courses.

The years flew by, yet every anniversary of Elaine's death brought me to the edge of the abyss. The trips back to Portland to lay flowers on her gravestone were the most difficult. After, I would walk around for days wrapped in a fog of numbness. Only the knowledge that with each passing day I was arming myself to fight her cancer lifted me from the darkness.

Unfortunately, Jeremy did not fare as well. The pain of Elaine's loss had taken longer to sink in, but when it did, it set him on a path of self-destructiveness. He started drinking until he was politely asked to take a leave of absence from work. I called him on several occasions, urging him to get help. But he shrugged it off, telling me he would be fine.

One night the phone rang, and I could hear Jeremy mumbling on the other end, inebriated. He informed me that he had finally realized that staying in Maine was the source of all his problems. At every turn, something reminded him of Elaine. His friend Philip, from Greece, had offered Jeremy his summerhouse on the island of Patmos for six months and he was calling to say goodbye. I asked him what he planned to do after the six months were over.

"I have no idea," he quipped. "That's why I'm going to Greece. So I can figure things out."

I wished him well, begging him to take care of himself.

"Good luck," he said as he hung up the phone. It was the last I would hear from him for many years.

In 2004, I graduated from Yale cum laude and was accepted at the Johns Hopkins Hospital for my residency in pediatric hematology. Moving cities again to work in such a prestigious institution gave me a real lift. But when I finally came face-to-face with my first patient, a young boy suffering from leukemia, all the armor I had built up around me came crumbling down. Seeing the hope and desperation in his parents' eyes put me right back at Elaine's bedside, where I had spent so many help-less nights watching over her.

As I monitored the boy's progress, it dawned on me that I was now standing on the other side of the proverbial fence. Instead of waiting hours to hear from doctors, I worked behind closed doors with the rest of his medical team, mapping every detail of his treatment. I was actively fighting his cancer, and that simple shift in perspective filled me with strength.

My first patient fared well. Soon after he completed his chemotherapy, we were able to declare him "No Evidence of Disease," or NED. Such a quick victory validated all of the efforts I had made to get this far. During a quiet moment in the cafeteria, while I was warming myself with a cup of tea, I suddenly felt Elaine's presence in the room as though she were celebrating alongside me. I've been standing too long on my feet, I thought to myself, quickly dismissing the experience.

Not every case would go so well. The time inevitably came when I had to cope with the death of one of my patients, a six-year-old girl named Jasmine. Her passing hit me hard, despite the efforts of my supervising physicians to remind me that death came with the territory in this line of work. When I cried along with her parents, I earned a rebuke for unprofessional behavior. Yet to my surprise, this new grief came with a silver lining for it allowed a little of my old pain to resurface. Reliving a child's journey through cancer was like watching a tragic movie for the second time. I was able to make better sense of all the twists and turns while, at the same time, experiencing a greater emotional distance. Helping others through their suffering had a definite healing effect, even if it brought with it a fresh dose of grief.

Unfortunately, misery only invited more misery. During the final months of my residency, I received a frantic call from my mother, who screamed through the receiver that my father had suffered a heart attack.

I got to the airport as fast as I could. As the plane's nose lifted and disappeared into the clouds, I thought about how he had changed since I had last hugged him goodbye. I knew my father had never fully recovered from the tragedy of Elaine's death. He had grown quiet and introverted over the years, letting most of his interests fall by the wayside, idling his time away with crossword puzzles. Although he had only recently turned sixty-one, he sold his practice to a young optometrist and took an early retirement. What nobody knew at the time was that my father was suffering from severe hypertension, which had gone undiagnosed because he had stopped going to his annual checkups. It was as if he had thrown his hands up and given up on life.

My mother, for her part, had weathered the storm of Elaine's passing with much greater equipoise. In the aftermath, she had helped my father through his depression and kept his business running. They purchased a condominium in Florida and began spending most of their winters there, which did him good.

When I arrived at the Maine Medical Center's emergency room, I found my mother in a chair, sobbing quietly. I crouched down and threw my arms around her. She gripped me tightly, as though she would never let go.

"Where's Dad?" I asked. But she just shook her head.

∾

Standing once again on the green lawn of the cemetery, the sight of my father's casket being lowered into the ground filled me with a terrible sense of helplessness and déjà vu. We could control so much in life, but we couldn't control the duration of our own existence—the one thing which mattered most.

As I listened to the prayers, that irritating age-old question surfaced in my mind. Do our fragile lives conceal a deeper purpose? There's no purpose to anything at all, my mind yelled back. But since I had been visited before by such nihilistic winds, I didn't give them too much thought. Instead, I just stood there, remembering my father and how much I loved him.

After it was over, I made my way back to my car with my arm around my mother's shoulders. Only the dead have seen the end of suffering, I thought to myself, altering Plato's famous maxim. On that point, I hadn't a shred of a doubt.

ANTHONY

$\mathcal{I}$t took time for me to digest the pain of my father's death, so I lowered my head and worked. Before I knew it, my residency was over. My dream of becoming a licensed physician had finally come true.

After saying goodbye to my mentors at Johns Hopkins, I headed north to begin a coveted three-year fellowship at the Dana-Farber/Boston Children's Cancer and Blood Disorders Center. There I would divide my time between patient care and clinical research in the latest cancer genomics in the fight against leukemia. I also hoped that I could stay in Boston, a city I loved, on a permanent basis since I had enough of moving around. With any luck, a job would be waiting for me once my fellowship was over.

If I was judged a workaholic in medical school, I had now become certifiably obsessed. I worked day and night and knew no life outside of the hospital. Yet despite the odds, I somehow managed to meet Anthony.

We met by chance at a cupcake shop a few blocks from the hospital. As I stood in line, I noticed a man picking up a dozen cupcakes for his daughter's birthday party. When they gave him the last lemon swirl, he politely offered it to me after he caught me staring at it.

"That's not necessary," I said. But he insisted, which I thought was a nice gesture.

Although he had a heavyset jaw, there was a softness in his eyes that told me he was caring. When he joked that we should meet again over cupcakes, I laughed and said, "Why not?"

"You're not serious?" he asked.

We set a date for the following week.

Anthony was a second-generation Italian whose parents had emigrated from Milan. It turned out we had a few things in common. To start, we had both experienced a death in the family. Almost six years ago, Anthony's wife, Debora, had died in a Jet Ski accident in Miami Beach. To make matters worse, Anthony had no idea at the time that his wife was in Florida. She was supposed to be in New York, attending a corporate training program, but had secretly escaped to Miami for the weekend with a colleague with whom she was having an affair. Her lover was racing their Jet Ski when he miscalculated a turn and slammed into a passing speedboat. She suffered severe head injuries, drowning before anyone could reach her. They rescued her lover, but he died on the way to the hospital.

As devastating as the double blow was to Anthony, it hurt his daughter even more. Claire was only eleven when the accident took place. When news of the affair finally reached her ears, she was not able to reconcile her anger while mourning her loss. She would wake up furious some mornings, blaming her mother for her own death. On other days, she felt guilty and wept because of how much she missed her. The constant seesaw of emotions dragged her into a deep depression.

Anthony understood her suffering and arranged for therapy. It appeared to help, at first, until Claire began acting out. Her grades dropped and she grew rebellious, breaking curfews and getting into all kinds of trouble. Two years later, Anthony discovered she was bulimic when he found her kneeling over the toilet with a finger down her throat. More therapy followed until she managed to pull herself together.

All of these details were revealed to me over a slice of pizza. Anthony spoke fast, waving his hands like a typical Italian, and I was moved by how open and honest he was. When he smiled, which was often, the wrinkles around his eyes made him look wise, giving me comfort. Like me, he had suffered an awful tragedy but managed to keep going. But unlike me, he had the responsibility of raising a teenage daughter while I only had myself to look after, which made me feel a tad self-absorbed.

"So tell me about your work," I said, sipping my wine.

"It's not very exciting. Do you know those little red and blue lights in home stereos and other electronics? They're called LED lights. I manufacture them."

"How wonderful!" I exclaimed, not knowing what else to say.

Anthony laughed. "For what it's worth, I'm proud the company is still kicking. I started it when I was just twenty-three, fresh out of Cornell engineering."

As we talked, Anthony did something that most men would never do on a first date. He revealed that his business had fallen on hard times under increasing pressure from China.

"I just can't compete with their low labor costs anymore."

"I'm sorry to hear that," I said.

Anthony shrugged. "I'm not too worried. Where there's a will, there's a way," he said, forcing a smile.

The fact that his company was struggling might have been a turnoff for most women. But instead of letting his financial problems scare me away, I looked beyond them. Deep inside I sensed that Anthony was a decent man, someone I could count on. And I figured that, in time, he would either turn things around or search for a new business opportunity.

~

I was nervous a few weeks later as I drove over to meet Claire. What would she think of me? When she walked into the room, I felt the weight of the world walking in with her.

"Hi, Claire. So nice to meet you."

She looked up at me and smiled, extending a limp hand.

Claire wasn't tall, around five foot two, with floppy black hair that made her naturally pale skin look even whiter. She spoke little at first, but over time she grew to accept my presence at the house.

As the weeks turned into months, Anthony and I grew close. Unlike Jeremy, who was a born idealist, Anthony didn't feel the need to try to right all of the world's wrongs. Instead, he prioritized everything around Claire, driving her to all her appointments and taking care of her every need. Like me, he rarely felt the need to go out. He was content during his free time to tinker in his toolshed or watch a Red Sox game. So while I might have dismissed him in my younger years as boring, his down-to-earth personality felt right this time.

After dating for almost a year, I closed my eyes and took the plunge. I moved out of my little condo near the Museum of Fine Arts into Anthony's four-bedroom house out in Needham. In truth, I already spent most of my time at his place, and the thought of playing a more permanent role in Claire's life appealed to me. I relished the chance to be a mother of sorts, even though Claire had already reached the stage where she preferred to be locked away in her room or plugged into her iPod.

When we floated the idea of my moving in over cheesecake, she shrugged.

"Sure," was all she bothered to say.

I smiled with the hope that, with a little more time and proximity, she would warm up to me.

DANA-FARBER

*A*utumn gave way to winter and, before I could blink, the house was covered with Christmas lights. Sitting by the fireplace with Anthony that New Year's Eve was sheer bliss. Everything had fallen back into harmony. Everything was once again in its rightful place.

"Happy New Year!" I sang, kissing him at the stroke of midnight.

By January, I had reached the halfway mark of my fellowship, and things were looking rosy. One afternoon, Dr. Brendan Connor, the Chair of the Pediatrics Department, walked up to me and asked if I would care to join him in his office.

"I have some news you might be interested in hearing," he whispered.

Dr. Connor was a legend around Dana-Farber's halls. A short man with curly blond hair and thin wire spectacles, he was regarded as one of the world's leading pediatric leukemia experts. His name had been associated with no fewer than ten major clinical trials and dozens of publications over the years which had ushered important advances into the field. His presence was one of the main reasons I was so thrilled I'd been invited to work at the Center.

He walked across his office, his fingers trailing over his glass desk, before he sank into his chair.

"Make yourself comfortable," he said. "I've been observing you since you joined us," he began, "and I think you're off to a good start.

"You may or may not be aware of this, but we've just been issued final IRB certification to begin a phase two trial of Navatinib," he said.

I was, of course, fully aware of the Center's anticipated projects.

"I've also heard from reliable sources that our colleagues in Basel plan to work on the same inhibitor we intend to examine in this trial."

He didn't need to say anything more. Although it was common practice to consult with other cancer experts around the world, the first to the finish line took the trophy when it came to publishing new science. Our colleagues in Switzerland were also our competition, and he was telling me that he had every intention to publish first.

Dr. Connor leaned forward and removed his glasses, instantly shedding a few years from his face.

"I want you to run the trials. Under my supervision, of course."

I couldn't believe what I was hearing.

"We'll co-publish."

Did he just say co-publish?

I wondered what I had done to deserve such an honor. Was it because of the long hours I put in, or did he feel sorry that I had lost my own child to cancer?

I put an end to the little voice of self-doubt yammering in my head. Maybe, just maybe, he had chosen me not out of pity but due to the quality of my work. Or had he?

There was my self-doubt again.

"You look lost."

I snapped out of my daze. "No," I said. "I just wasn't expecting such a privilege."

"Well, we're ramping up on a tight schedule, so please read everything there is to know on the BMI-1 gene."

The BMI-1 gene was a cancer stem cell regulator which played a central part in allowing the propagation of leukemia cells. Shutting it down prevented cancer cells from replicating, effectively stopping them in their tracks. Now that we had it in our crosshairs, if the human trials of this new Navatinib drug went well, it would open the door to new therapies that could save thousands of young lives.

As I drove home that evening, I couldn't believe my luck. The trial had been allocated special funding by the National Cancer Institute. That alone improved my chances of a permanent job offer once my fellowship was over.

I pulled into Anthony's driveway and killed the engine. But instead of running into the house to share the news, I sat in my car biting my nails and organizing urgent to-do lists in my mind. It was clear that I had my work cut out for me.

CLAIRE

*M*oving in with Anthony didn't turn out quite as I had expected. For the first month at least, every-thing was blissful. The dynamic of a new person in the house lent itself to a honeymoon atmosphere. We were all polite, help-ful, and extra considerate around each other. But as the weeks went by, and we settled back into our patterns and rhythms, the edges of our personalities began to rub against each other.

The tensions that surfaced were, thankfully, not between Anthony and me. They only involved Claire. As I got to know her better, I saw that her problems ran deeper than I had initially perceived. I realized she had never really emerged from the depression caused by her mother's death; she had just learned how to mask it. It fueled her low self-esteem and general lack of ambition. But even more troubling was how she used her sadness as an excuse to justify her behavior.

When I shared my thoughts with Anthony, he became defensive.

"You're overanalyzing," he said.

"And you're ignoring a problem that's not going to fix itself," I responded.

A few days later, I suggested that Claire go back into therapy, but Anthony mumbled something about the high cost of each session.

"Don't worry," I said. "I'll take care of it."

Claire didn't appreciate learning that she was going back to the psychologist on my behalf. After the first few sessions, she grew even more rebellious and withdrawn. When we switched her to a different therapist, she hated the new one even more than the first.

One night, while staring into a glass of wine, I wondered if there was anything more I could do to help, even though my free time was almost nonexistent. Still, I decided to get even more involved in her life. I helped her with her homework, took her out shopping, even watched movies together over bowls of popcorn. In short, I did everything possible to win her heart and give her nothing less than the feeling that she had a mother again.

I thought things were moving in the right direction until Claire waltzed into the kitchen one Sunday morning and announced she no longer had any intentions of applying to college.

"I'm following my dream to become a photographer," she said. "I'm applying to the New England School of Photography. Bye-bye SATs," she smirked.

A terrible argument erupted, Anthony and I attacking her lack of foresight. How could she even think of throwing away a university education, especially one which was already funded to the tune of over one hundred thousand dollars? It was a slap in her father's face, made worse since the money had come from her mother's life insurance payout. I forgot for a second that she wasn't my daughter, and I launched into a speech about how opting out of college was the stupidest thing she could ever do.

We cycled through all the standard arguments. What would

she do if she failed as a photographer or discovered she didn't like it after all? She would be left with nothing while missing out on a life-changing experience. What if she loved it but struggled in the future to make ends meet? She would have to settle for a life of menial work.

"You could study photography on the side while earning your bachelor's degree," I reminded her.

Yet however hard we tried, Claire was deaf to our reasoning.

"What about all that crap about following your dreams?" she said to her father. "Even if I hate it or end up a big failure, I'm still young enough to go back and get your stupid bachelor's degree," she screamed. Then she shot me a dirty look and stormed out of the house, slamming the door so hard that I thought a window would break.

MOTHERHOOD

$\mathcal{W}$e stood in the kitchen for a while without saying a word, letting the post-argument silence calm us down. When I turned to Anthony, he looked unnerved.

"Maybe I'm being too hard on her," he said.

I was surprised to hear this, so I assumed he just felt bad for his daughter. I expected Anthony to set Claire straight, but, as we spoke, it became clear he was considering allowing her to skip college against his own better judgment, which led to another argument between us.

"What about the life insurance money?"

"I'll use it to pay for whatever photography program she decides to attend," he said. "The rest I'll use to cover her rent until she finds a job."

I shook my head in disbelief. I had never seen this side of Anthony.

Over the next few days, I tried to understand what was going on in that house. Why would Anthony let his daughter walk all over him, especially on matters so vital to her future? Then it dawned on me that Anthony was as frightened as Claire. The shock and trauma of her mother's death had made

Claire as fragile as a crystal glass, or at least that's what Anthony believed. To protect her from further conflict, he had allowed her to grow selfish and irreverent. Anthony worried that any more pressure on his daughter would send her careening over the edge. But I saw it differently. I was convinced that what she needed more than anything was a strong hand to steer her back in the right direction.

I explained my theories to Anthony several times until he admitted that what I said made sense. And yet, despite his repeated promises to stick to his principles and reverse his decision, nothing came of it. Claire continued doing whatever she pleased, while Anthony imposed only the lightest of punishments.

After our fight, things never returned to normal between Claire and me. We spent less and less time together, to the point where I felt she was avoiding me. Although I had given it my best, it was obvious that I had failed to bond with Claire in any significant way. I had no choice except to acknowledge that my second attempt at motherhood was proving to be a failure.

TINY CRACKS

*T*he launch of the clinical trial drew me deep into my work. As Dr. Connor's co-investigator, I was tasked with a long list of competing priorities, from preparing clinical binders to liaising with the IRB and NCI to talking to the data manager umpteen times a day. Not to mention the heart-breaking job of sitting and holding hands with my toddler patients. All of it translated into even longer hours tucked away in my small office, often well into the night. Though the trial was just getting off its feet, we were rushing to write an introductory paper that would throw us into the spotlight before our friends in Europe had a chance to publish.

During those first months, Dr. Connor sat with a group of us in his office, holding court with a large cup of coffee in one hand while flipping through case reports with the other, searching for errors. He would sometimes lift his head and smile, while at other times he barked out questions that sent us scrambling for answers. On other occasions, we just sat in silence while he scribbled notes on a yellow pad. But even then, he radiated a palpable intensity that kept us all on edge.

At home, Anthony's business troubles were only getting

worse. His sales continued to slide, but he was unable to reduce his prices any further. It was a difficult situation, especially for the people who worked for him. While he considered the possibility of selling the business, laying off more staff, or even trying to manufacture a different product, he was unwilling in the end to rethink or let go of the company he had worked so hard to build. So he just poured money into marketing and advertising, hoping to convince potential customers that his products were better than the cheap imitations from China.

The decline in Anthony's fortunes led to some unexpected consequences. As money grew tighter, slowly, but surely, I began covering the shortfall. I found myself paying for things that Anthony would have never let me pay for before, such as a new water heater for the house or Claire's latest cavity filling. Not that I minded helping out. In fact, I enjoyed it. But what surprised me was the sudden change in dynamic between us. I knew something was up when I forgot one afternoon that Anthony was planning to watch a Patriots game, and I asked him to drive me to Boylston Street. Instead of speaking up, he just bit his lip and motioned for us to go. Only when we were halfway there did I realize he was so quiet because he was upset I had disrupted his game watching.

"Why didn't you remind me?" I asked, but he just shrugged his shoulders and said it was no big deal.

Similar incidents occurred with greater frequency. While standing in line at the bank, I reminded him that he had no reason to feel ashamed just because I was helping the family out.

"Yes, yes," he replied with a wave of his hand, trying to hide his embarrassment.

Anthony's odd behavior and Claire's coolness toward me caused me to seek shelter in the only way I knew, by disappearing even deeper into my work. Inside I lamented the fact that I would never play the role of mother I so wanted. I had come to the difficult realization that it was impossible for me to love Claire in the way that I had hoped, for part of loving a child rests in one's ability to shape them in your image, however selfish that might sound. As far as I could tell, Claire's essence had already taken a shape I could never change. Or it required enormous amounts of time and energy to fix, both of which I didn't have.

Cracks at home began to show. I caught myself losing my temper and being curt, even condescending, at times. But instead of standing up to me when I was too hard on Claire, Anthony just stood on the sidelines, comforting his daughter only when he thought I was out of earshot. Without question, this wasn't the same Laura McDermott I was proud to be, and I regretted that the money situation had caused Anthony to feel emasculated around me.

THE DIAGNOSIS

*S*uch were the little dramas playing out in my life when I was hit with my cancer diagnosis.

It happened almost without warning. In hindsight, I do recall a few restless nights where I woke up cold and sweaty at the same time, but I thought it was just stress. I knew something was up when I got up one morning and discovered a large lump in my neck just above my right clavicle. I quickly made an appointment to see my family doctor. When I mentioned it over lunch with Dr. Connor, he reached over the table to touch it.

"I agree. This needs to be looked at."

"I'm seeing Meredith Friday morning."

"Ah, yes, send her my regards," he added.

Dr. Connor rapped his knuckles on the table. "You know, I just remembered that we have a conference call with Dr. Epstein set up for this Friday at eight thirty. We need to determine how any adverse reactions will affect the study."

He sat there, waiting for me to say something until my awareness of being a subordinate kicked in.

"Not a problem. I'll reschedule my appointment," I said.

"Very good," he replied, digging his fork into his pasta.

In truth, I didn't mind delaying my appointment. I figured my swollen lymph node was nothing more than a reaction to a canker sore or an infected tooth. Standing before my bathroom mirror, I inspected my mouth with the help of a flashlight but couldn't find anything amiss. I touched my neck. The lump itself was not painful, just tender.

I finally made it to my doctor the following Wednesday, who sent me for a blood test and neck x-ray. When the results proved inconclusive, she referred me to an ear, neck, and throat specialist at Massachusetts General Hospital. After a quick checkup, he decided that a pathologist should perform a fine needle biopsy of the lump, which still showed no signs of going down.

Of course, by this point, I knew something was seriously wrong. Lymph nodes don't stay swollen for that long without good reason.

During the five days I awaited my results, the inevitable rumors began to swirl. Everyone at work knew I was walking around with a lump on my neck and, since we were cancer specialists, we all knew what it could mean. As for me, I clung to the hope that I was carrying some kind of persistent bacterial infection since the alternatives looming in the dark were much more sinister.

Finally, on the 16th of April 2009, a call came from the ENT's office urging me to come down as fast as possible.

I jumped into my car and raced through the streets, telling myself the entire time that whatever I had was fixable. When I pulled into the hospital's parking lot, it took me a good five minutes of driving around in circles before I found a spot, which almost gave me a fit.

I ran through the lobby, barely squeezing into an elevator. I exited on the third floor and followed the signs until I stood before door 35H. As I raised my fist to give it a knock, I was overcome by the terrible feeling that I was about to step into a nightmare.

The door opened, and we shook hands. Dr. Mayhew was a tall man who had gone bald, except for a swath of silver hair above the ears. His open hand pointed to a worn brown leather chair.

"Please, have a seat," he said. He sank into the opposite chair and swung a leg over his knee.

I sat down, trying to catch my breath.

Dr. Mayhew straightened his back and entwined his fingers. He gazed at me with a semi-blank stare, and, by his tone and body language, I knew without question that he was about to deliver a cancer diagnosis.

"Look, I'm afraid the news could be better. It's melanoma."

I sat in his examination room, stunned. My mind drew a blank and, for a moment, I forgot where I was. Then I remembered Elaine and all she had suffered, and how I had vowed to fight her cancer as hard as I could. But now another cancer was attacking me, which made me feel like the victim of a cruel joke.

"Melanoma?" I said. "But how's that possible? I've spent my entire life in snowy New England, except for my residency in Baltimore."

He looked at me and shook his head. "We're seeing a lot of cases coming from places we normally don't expect. We're not sure why."

A wave of anger welled up inside me, causing a few teardrops to roll down my face.

"I'm sorry," Dr. Mayhew continued. "It's quite advanced inside your lymph node, so we need to locate the primary tumor to determine if it has spread to any other organs."

I knew how things worked and exactly what would follow, including the MRI, CAT, and PET scans that would search for additional tumors.

Instead of booking another appointment, Dr. Mayhew arranged for me to be scanned that same day. I lay still for what felt like hours, listening to the hum of the machines. They examined every inch of my body, searching for clusters of malignant cells. When I saw the results, I held my breath in disbelief. The cancer was metastatic. It had spread to my thyroid, left lung, and had descended into my bowels, which meant I was officially at stage IV. Life expectancy was grim. I had five to twenty months, give or take, to live.

After the diagnosis, I was in no condition to drive, so Anthony came to pick me up. I sat stone-faced while he uttered the usual comforting platitudes about how we would fight it, that it might not be as bad as it looked, and so on. Everything I told Jeremy when Elaine was first diagnosed. But behind his calm facade, I could sense that he was nervous.

As I stared out the car window, the passing city oblivious to my pain, I could not accept that I had gone from rising cancer specialist to dying patient in a flash. Even more frustrating, I had not suffered any symptoms apart from the short bout of night sweats and the swollen lymph node. Beyond that, there had been no pain, no dizziness, and no fatigue. Nothing to signal that I was so sick.

When we pulled up alongside the Charles River, my emotions unraveled. I cupped my hands to my face and sobbed.

"It's okay, honey. We're going to get through this together," he said, placing his hand on my knee.

Despite Anthony's assurances, I knew that my body had betrayed me. What he didn't understand was that if melanoma isn't caught early, it's usually fatal. When we arrived home, Anthony went upstairs to talk to Claire while I sat on the living room sofa, still feeling heavy and disoriented, still hoping to wake up at any given moment.

I didn't move for a few minutes, aware of nothing except the sound of my breath. The cordless phone hanging on the kitchen wall looked as if it were staring at me. I stood up, walked across the room, and picked up the receiver, hesitating for a second before dialing my mother's number.

With the ringtone sounding in my ear, I imagined how the news would affect her. In life, children are supposed to outlive their parents. She had already suffered from the death of both her granddaughter and her husband. Now there was a real possibility she would have to bear witness to my own passing, her one and only child.

I hung up the phone, not knowing how I would find the strength to break such terrible news. A dint of hope flashed in my mind that whatever cancer treatment I undertook would deliver a miracle, sparing her from learning of my diagnosis, at least for the time being. So when the phone rang five minutes later with my mother on the other end, I lied to her. I told her everything was fine, and that I had just called to say hello.

After our goodbyes, I leaned against the kitchen island and pressed my palms into my eyes, trying my best to hold back a fresh wave of tears.

WELL WISHES

*T*he cancer inside me was like a ticking bomb. Since time was of the essence, I met with the oncology team at Mass General the very next morning. Dr. Juro Yoshimura, a melanoma specialist, would serve as my lead oncologist. He was a well-respected physician who was also a faculty member at Harvard. His eyes sparkled when he spoke, and every few sentences he flashed a smile that could put even the most nervous patient at ease.

Since I was also a cancer physician, the discussion of my options proceeded unconventionally. Instead of telling me what was best, Dr. Yoshimura and I reviewed the latest therapies together as colleagues until we settled on an aggressive mix of chemotherapy and immunotherapy treatments. They would run for five cycles, a total of fifteen weeks, with the hope of pushing my melanoma into remission.

The protocol was designed to act as a pincer movement. On the one hand, the chemotherapy would destroy or shrink the tumor cells, while on the other, the immunotherapy would stimulate my immune system to better fight the cancer. Even though alternatives existed, we both knew that the initial rounds of treatment had to produce significant results for me to live for years instead of months.

When I got back to the house, I ran to the toilet to throw up, but nothing came out. I wondered if the tumors in my body were making me feel ill or if just the thought of knowing I had cancer was to blame. I lay down on my bed while Anthony ran a hot bath for me, and, for all of his good intentions, I could see that he was still struggling to come to terms with the sudden turn of events. On the upside, if there could be an upside, all the squabbles and lingering tension between us simply evaporated. Claire, on the other hand, began acting stranger than ever around me, wavering between showing empathy and outright ignoring me, the clear lines of our relationship now blurred since I had fallen victim, like her, to circumstances beyond my control.

The next morning, I met privately with Dr. Connor in his office before breaking the news to the rest of the floor. As he listened to my diagnosis, he pressed the tips of his fingers into a triangle and nodded with an expression of utmost concern.

"I'm deeply sorry to hear this terrible news," he said.

"Me, too." I smiled.

He reached over the desk to grab my hand. "Laura, you know I'm going to be with you every step of the way," he said as if talking to one of his own patients.

"Thank you," I replied.

"When do you begin treatment?"

"Intake starts on Friday with the first cycle scheduled for Monday."

By intake, I meant the battery of tests I had to undergo to determine if my body was strong enough to handle the biochemotherapy, which came with ravaging side effects.

Dr. Connor leaned back into his chair.

"It goes without saying that you've become an exceptional member of our department," he began. "And we both know how much progress we've made over the last three months."

I nodded.

"First, I'd like to say I'm sorry you won't be able to join me in Philly. I know how hard you worked on the paper. You deserve to be there."

By Philly he meant the keynote speech he was going to deliver at the annual meeting at the American Society of Pediatric Hematology/Oncology in Philadelphia. We were excited to present our findings, which would serve as a prelude to the final peer-reviewed paper that the Dana-Farber Cancer Center would submit to the leading medical journal, *The Lancet*, after our clinical trial closed.

"Well, at least the first one is ready," I said.

"Yes, and it reads beautifully, so thank you," he replied.

Dr. Connor leaned over to me, smiling. "You know, I have a feeling you're going to be all right. I think before you know it, you'll be back at work. I'm sure your name will be in the abstract when we publish. In fact, I insist it be there," he exclaimed.

"I sure hope so," I replied, allowing myself to believe what he was saying. To become published alongside Dr. Connor so early in my career, and in such a prestigious journal, was the equivalent of being nominated for an Academy Award after acting in your first movie. In my heart of hearts, I hoped I would be well enough after my chemo to work on the trial's final paper.

Dr. Connor emailed our group that afternoon, sharing the news of my diagnosis. Within minutes, my inbox flooded with messages. A stream of people dropped by my office, expressing their disbelief, offering me hugs, wishing me well. A few of my closest colleagues made no effort to hide their tears. They were in absolute shock that I was at stage IV. Looking back, I was also in denial. Even though I knew what was happening and was planning for the battle like a general preparing for war, it hadn't registered in my mind that I might be dying. That realization would only come much later.

12

THE GLEAMING CROSS

I spent the weekend at Mass General being put
through the paces of the initial tests. The first procedure was an inch-by-inch full body examination to locate the
mole which had morphed into a tumor, the source of my
melanoma. But the point of origin was never found, and they
classified me with a cancer of unknown primary.

At 7:00 a.m., I checked in to the hospital to begin my first
cycle. Anthony and I were led to the private room that would
serve as my home for the next seven days. Arrangements had
been made for Claire to spend the week with her friend
Danielle, though we worried about the trouble she might
get into.

I brought little else besides my laptop, knowing that the
cocktail of chemo and biological agents would take the wind
out of me. I had witnessed the suffering of my little patients as
they went through their treatments, and now I repeated to
myself all the encouraging lies I used to tell them.

After settling in, Anthony went off to learn how to care for
the central venous catheter that would be inserted into my
chest, while I, in turn, was wheeled down for a final chest x-ray.

Back in the room, all we could do was wait for the bags of chemo to be delivered.

My treatment officially began just after 1:00 p.m. The line was plugged in, and for the next five hours, the drugs dripped slowly into my body. Tylenol and Demerol were administered to combat the onset of fever and chills.

I dreaded the next seven days, knowing how difficult they would be. Nurses would come in and weigh me every few hours to measure my fluid retention, as well as poking me for blood and checking my vitals. The monitoring would continue around the clock, disrupting my sleep. I was also instructed to breathe into a spirometer from time to time to prevent fluid from collecting in my lungs, which could lead to pneumonia. But beyond these intrusions, what bothered me the most was knowing that I wouldn't have the energy to get up and take a shower.

I sat up on my bed and glanced at the chemo bag hanging from the pole. As I observed the poison dripping into my bloodstream, memories of Elaine's suffering flashed in my mind, triggering a minor anxiety attack. I turned my head and saw Anthony staring out the window, lost in his thoughts. Not wanting to alarm him, I closed my eyes and tried to think of nothing.

To my great relief, the first three days turned out much better than I expected. Despite running a constant low-grade fever, I was able to sleep and eat and even spend quality time with Anthony away from Claire. In fact, I felt so normal I started to think there was something wrong with my drip. But my optimism was short-lived. As the hours ticked by, a dry-mouthed fatigue crept over me. I fell into long bouts of sleep, lost my appetite, and had to force myself to drink lots of water to fight the onset of chemical dehydration.

On the fourth night, my condition took a turn for the worse. I became severely nauseated almost without notice and had to be given a drug to level it off. Terrible stomach cramps followed, forcing me to run to the toilet again and again. When I woke up in the morning, I was sweating profusely and felt extremely weak. My eyeballs ached as if they were on fire, and I experienced constant tingling in my fingers and toes.

By the fifth day, my skin had turned bright red and became itchy, a side effect of the immune response drug. They moved me to a higher dosage of anti-nausea medication, which knocked me out and left me feeling like I had been run over by a truck. I slept for hours on end, and only in the early evening did I find the energy to let my nurse help me to a shower.

The following two days were recovery days. Instead of chemo, I was put on a potassium drip and given a glycoprotein injection to help replenish my white blood cells. I drank gallons of water and tried to walk as much as possible, but I never managed to stray too far from my bed.

Anthony had been more than wonderful throughout the entire week. He had slept on a half-broken reclining chair and attended to my needs without as much as whispering a complaint. When he smiled, I felt nothing but love and gratitude.

As the seventh and final day of my first chemo cycle drew to a close, I propped myself up on my pillow.

"I feel like I've been here forever," I said.

Anthony stood up to stretch. "I'll run you a hot bath as soon as we get home."

"I'm so tired you might have to carry me," I half-joked.

"Anytime," he said. As he sat down I noticed, through the window behind him, a church spire reaching high above the rooftops. A thin cross at the top of the spire sparkled against the dying sun, catching my attention.

"More water?" Anthony asked. But I didn't bother to respond; my eyes transfixed on the gleaming cross and the orange-tinged clouds floating past it.

1 3

THE STONE CHURCH

*H*ome never felt so good. Anthony and Claire had set up a small table with a nice plate of muffins, fresh cut fruit, and a jug of coffee with a Welcome Home sign above it. They had even tied a few balloons to both ends of the table.

As much as I wanted to stay, I grabbed a muffin and slowly made my way up the steps to shower and lie down. My skin itched beyond belief, and I was in desperate need of an antihistamine and some moisturizing cream. Exhausted, the drive had caused my nausea to return. But I was glad to be home.

I slept for most of the week. On Tuesday, Anthony drove me back to the hospital so I could take the twice-a-week blood test that was needed to monitor my platelet and white blood cell counts. If the numbers proved too low, I would require a transfusion. Thankfully, the results came back within the acceptable range. I also underwent new scans to measure the state of my tumors with the hope that some, if not all, would exhibit a high degree of shrinkage. The scans also searched for undetected tumors, a possibility I was terrified to consider.

By the second week, I felt much better since my nausea had lifted and my skin had, for the most part, stopped itching, though it was peeling as if from a sunburn. I was able to be up and around for most of the day and joined the family around the dinner table.

Since he saw that I was doing so well, Anthony agreed to let me drive myself to the hospital for my next blood test so he could catch up with some urgent business. When I arrived at the blood lab, I was told to expect a delay of at least an hour and a half.

I sat in the waiting room, flipping through a magazine before reminding myself to minimize my exposure to germs since the chemo had reduced my immune system to practically nothing. I put the magazine down and looked around until my knees began to fidget. Outside, the long Boston winter had finally melted away, and I wanted nothing more than to breathe in the warm spring air and bite into something sweet. I told myself that as long as I didn't stray too far from the hospital, I'd be okay.

I stepped into the sunshine and let the cool breeze caress my face, soothing me, filling me with energy. I walked across the parking lot, hoping to find a bakery. I crossed a couple of blocks and ended up in a residential street, only to find myself gazing at a small stone church standing in the center of a small park. When I looked up, I realized that I was standing before the same church whose spire I had seen from the hospital room window.

Panting, I sat down on a sidewalk bench to catch my breath. A bronze plaque on the stone wall in front of me read "The Church of Saint John of the Cross, erected 1897." I didn't give it much thought. I was about to walk away, when I noticed the church's main wooden door was ajar, and it was then that I felt an intense pull to step inside. I resisted the urge and checked my watch. I still had an hour to go before the nurse would see me.

I sat there for the next few minutes, basking in the warm

sunlight and enjoying the beauty of the old door, with its small cracks and worn-out bolts when it occurred to me that I couldn't remember the last time I had set foot in a house of worship.

Then, without notice, I experienced a strange and unexpected peace within me. It was a calm like I had never felt before, much different from the peace that comes from everyday life such as one might feel after completing a stressful exam. This peace was of a different order, and it beckoned me into the church. Unable to ignore it any longer, I stood up and pushed the door open to let myself through.

I allowed my eyes to adjust for a few moments and looked around. The first thing I noticed was the large lifelike statue of Jesus, hanging from the cross, his head tilted to his right, the red blood from his wounds clearly visible. The sweet fragrance of frankincense and myrrh filled the air, as if the thurible had just been walked through the nave, but the church appeared completely empty. There was not a soul in sight.

I walked past the brass fount of holy water and sat in one of the pews. A slight odor of varnish lifted from the wood, reminding me of attending Mass with my mother as a young girl.

The church itself was sparse, the walls nothing except bare gray stone. To the sides and behind the altar rose Gothic-shaped windows of stained glass, depicting various saints and figures. The altar itself was elegant and simple, a long wooden table covered by a white cloth with two large candles at both ends. Behind it, against the back of the sepulchrum, stood a white marble table with the tabernacle at its center and two porcelain flower vases on either side.

Cut into the walls on both aisles were oval niches housing plaster statues of saints who I couldn't hope to name. On the aisle to my left, centered between two statues, stood a large wooden confessional. It was a solid oak structure adorned with elaborate carvings, giving it a regal look. Beyond that, it was like any other I had seen: a simple square box with two compartments to either side of the priest's area, each with a door to safeguard privacy, with three light bulbs affixed to the top of the structure—a green light at the center to indicate the priest was present, and red lights over the left and right compartments to signal a penitent was inside.

As I stared at the confessional, the green light over the priest's door lit up. Strange, I thought to myself, since I had not seen anyone step inside.

I watched the light for some time, reliving with disdain the few times I had submitted to confession as a teenager. It was one of the many aspects of the Church that bothered me, this idea of confessing my most private thoughts and behaviors to a strange man whom I felt was judging me. Since I didn't believe in God, I always suspected that the priest took some kind of perverse pleasure in hearing me confess my so-called sins, some of which I didn't think were sins at all.

Sitting there now, though, in the midst of fighting my cancer and after losing Elaine, filled me with an unexpected sense of nostalgia. A tinge of sadness washed over me, and I thought it might be nice to listen once again to a priest's whispering voice. I glanced at my watch. Seeing that I still had some time to kill, I pushed my prejudices aside and stood up to make my way to the confessional.

THE FIRST VISIT

*W*hen I stepped into the booth, I was relieved to find a small chair next to the kneeler since I was in no condition to kneel. As I sat down, I sensed the presence of the priest behind the grille. I remained quiet, listening to my own breath, and noticed that the small space felt unusually cold. I crossed my arms to keep warm, which made me feel like a schoolgirl.

I already wanted to leave.

Then the priest spoke. "May the Lord who resides in your heart guide you to a good confession."

It was a firm, yet soft, voice. Not the voice of an old man, but of someone close to my age, perhaps a man in his forties.

I made the sign of the cross and uttered, "Bless me, Father, for I have sinned. It has been more than—"

I stopped, searching my memory for when I had last gone to confession.

"—it's been more than twenty years since my last confession."

I fell silent, unable to speak.

"My child, will you not confess your sins?" he asked.

All of a sudden I felt stupid sitting in that confessional, like a complete fraud.

"Father, I'm sorry for wasting your time," I blurted out. "I shouldn't have come here."

"Why not?" he asked.

I hesitated for a second. "What's the point of confessing if you don't believe in God?"

I regretted the words as soon as they left my mouth. Embarrassed, I waited for his rebuke until I was met by the sensation that he was smiling on the other side.

"Well, you have confessed your first sin," he replied. "But don't fear. God still believes in you."

The softness of his answer took me by surprise.

"That's very kind of you, Father," I said, trying to be polite.

"It's not kindness. Just the truth," he said.

To my surprise that statement, uttered with such confidence, caused all of my old anger to flare up. The fact-finding scientist in me decided to rear her obstinate head.

"Father, before I confess my sins, may I ask you a few questions?"

I heard what sounded like a sigh. "If you ask, my child, I shall be bound to answer as best as I can."

"Thank you," I said. "I don't mean to be blunt, but what makes you so sure God exists?"

"My child, asking if God exists is like the mouth asking whether the tongue exists."

Although his answer was witty, it didn't satisfy me in the least.

"How so?" I asked.

"God dwells in the heart. That's why He's said to be closer to you than your own breath, but you must have faith that He exists. When your faith grows strong enough, you'll be able to feel His presence."

"But that's my problem," I replied. "Convincing myself that

something exists doesn't make it true. For me to believe in something requires some form of evidence."

There was a long silence, as if he were deciding how to address my particular type of mind.

"You should first understand that nothing objective can prove His existence since God is not an object of knowledge. God is the source of all knowledge. If He could be proven on the outside, like an object under a microscope, He would be a lesser being. But God is the Supreme Being. Nothing exists outside of God."

"So he can never be proven," I said.

"Not in the way that you think, but there is a way," he said.

"How?"

"You have to deepen your understanding. You have to begin by accepting that what you understand to be God is a childish fantasy."

"The father figure with a white beard, up in heaven?" I said.

"Yes, exactly."

"God," he continued, "is hidden in your own sense of being."

"In what way?"

"My child, you know without a doubt that you exist from moment to moment. That feeling of being present has to come from somewhere. Only nothing comes from nothing." He repeated the words slowly, to make sure I got the point. "Only nothing comes from nothing."

This was the creationist argument. The universe must have been created from something or someone because it couldn't have sprung out of nothing, but it went against my Darwinian training.

"Your sense of being, your consciousness," he continued, "must rise from somewhere just as a wave rises from the ocean or a sunray from the sun. In the same way, your own self-awareness is the secret proof that God exists, for you are nothing except a reflection within God's eternal being."

"What do you mean by a reflection in God's being?"

"Consider the surface of a mirror, and what is reflected within. All of the objects reflected in the mirror require the mirror's surface in order for them to be seen, but objects do not affect the mirror in any way. Likewise, all objects are created and reflected within God's being, but they can't affect God in any way."

"But the objects in a mirror are actually outside the mirror."

"Yes, that's true. So the analogy is less than perfect. In the case of God's creation, everything materializes within God's being and is illumined only by God's light," he said.

"Like the images that appear on a TV screen," I offered.

"Yes, exactly. They are contained within the screen but don't affect the screen in any way.

"God is nothing except pure being, pure awareness," he continued. "He is the awareness that precedes time and space. He is the awareness that is unchanging, ever-present. Since there isn't any place where God is not present, he must also be present within you. If you ask where, it's in the form of your own awareness, your most subtle part. So the final truth is that there is no difference between God and your innermost being. They are one and the same."

I remained silent for a moment, absorbing what he had said. It was not what I expected to hear from a Catholic priest. But even to my faded memory of the Bible, this didn't sound anything like the far away, angry God of the Old Testament. I did, however, remember something from Genesis. The part where the serpent promised Eve that if she ate the fruit from the forbidden tree, she would be like God and become divine. Wasn't that the serpent's deception, to tell humans they could also be divine?

I voiced this objection just to hear what he had to say.

"Well," he began, "what I'm going to say may anger our evangelical brothers and sisters, but the truth is that parts of the Old Testament are metaphorical. None other than Saint Augustine in his book of Confessions argued this point, and few have possessed his depth of study. The story of the serpent teaches that humans should be humble before the Lord's infinite wisdom. It also teaches that to be human means, by definition, to have limited understanding. An ordinary human being does not possess God's omniscience. The moral of the passage is not that humans aren't divine, but, given his obvious and limited condition, a human being should not fall prey to pride and delusions of grandeur."

"So, are humans divine or not?" I asked.

"How can they not be when God exists within them, and they exist within God? What part of you is separate from God, I ask? However, humans are not divine to the extent they remain unaware of their own divinity.

"When Adam and Eve ate from the tree of knowledge of good and evil, and became aware of their own nakedness, what the Bible is teaching is that the moment man became aware of his own individuality, he lost his innate identification with the Lord. In other words, Adam's original sin, the fall from grace, is a reference to the veiling of the knowledge of one's own divinity."

"I'm not sure I follow."

"Listen, the casting out from Eden is a metaphor for God dividing Himself into the universe to become human beings and all other things. Through His own freedom and infinite will, God caused Himself to forget His undivided nature and eternal existence as pure being. The moment He became aware of Himself as a limited human being was the so-called moment when Adam and Eve ate the fruit from the tree of knowledge of good and evil. It's the moment the Lord, within each person, identified Himself as a temporal mind and body instead of the pure awareness that is the eternal witness behind the mind and body."

The priest stopped to clear his throat. Even though I had never heard anyone speak such things, I was having trouble taking him seriously.

"Father, I'm not the most learned Catholic. But if I hear you correctly, you are saying that human beings are, in essence, not different than God. It sounds almost heretical in nature."

"Well, it might sound that way. But the real sin is distorting, misunderstanding, or even ignoring the teachings of Christ and His apostles. I'm only telling you what I know to be true."

"If God is undivided awareness, as you say, why would he choose to divide himself into the universe and forget himself by becoming human?"

"That's a most difficult question. One answer is that you'll have to wait to find out for yourself, once you've evolved spiritually and have regained your God-awareness. Another answer is that God went through the trouble of creating the universe, dividing Himself and concealing Himself from Himself simply for the joy of rediscovering Himself."

"So it's like a game of hide-and-seek that God plays with himself, if I can put it that way."

"That's a bit simplistic, but yes. A great being once said that the sole purpose of the human mind is to transcend itself. Likewise, the final use of the human body is to discard any use for a body."

"Father, coming back to what you first said about how my self-awareness is somehow proof of God's existence, I just can't accept that our consciousness is somehow special in any way, much less divine. It's nothing except the chemical and electrical firings in our brains. As a matter of fact, I happen to be a medical doctor. I've seen patients with severe brain injuries whose consciousness was severely compromised or no longer present."

"Yes, it's a great misunderstanding," he replied. "The idea that consciousness is a product of the human brain is a stubborn point of ignorance."

I was put off by his sense of certainty, even by what I would call his arrogance.

"Think of a small radio," he began. "If the radio works well, the electromagnetic waves will amplify through its speakers with clarity. But if some part of the radio is broken, the sound may come out distorted or there may not be any sound at all. That doesn't mean the waves in the air don't exist through and beyond the radio. In the same way, awareness is ever-present. But in a body that's broken, it may appear as though awareness is gone. As long as awareness is tied to the body through the breath, the life energy, awareness will appear to be affected by the body."

"But what about in a person who's dead?" I asked. "Where is their immortal awareness?"

"That's a good question," he said. "When a person dies, their awareness departs from the physical body through the soul, the body of light. Once the breath stops, the soul separates from the body. So the individual awareness in the form of the soul moves around. Even then, though, God's pure awareness is still behind the corpse, for not even an atom can exist if it's not supported by God's being."

"That's interesting," I said. "But I find it hard to believe that the empty space between us is filled with an awareness of some kind."

"Yes, the primary illusion behind creation is that we are points of awareness which are surrounded by inanimate objects. And in one way it's true. These objects are indeed inanimate, but that doesn't mean there's not any awareness behind them. Think of a white movie screen. An entire landscape with sky, trees, road, and people is projected onto the screen. And though you can't see the screen, the entire scene could not exist without the presence of the screen behind every inch of the image. The people in the scene are talking and have minds, while the rock on the ground is just a rock, but the white screen remains unseen behind both rock and person at all times."

"If awareness is everywhere, how can inanimate objects like a chair or a rock exist?"

"You are confusing awareness with possession of a mind. Awareness is the source of all minds, but it's not the endless stream of thoughts and intellect which we call the mind. For example, you are aware of what you are thinking at this moment. That awareness is separate from your thoughts. Your thoughts, in fact, appear as objects before your awareness. This is the same awareness which is one with God, and the same awareness which is behind the mind and behind all of creation, even the chair. Without that awareness, there would be nothing present to even know that thoughts exist. So be careful not to confuse the mind with pure awareness."

"But aren't thoughts aware of themselves?"

"No. Thoughts are combinations of sounds, and those sounds do not have any innate awareness. They're no different than any other inanimate object. Sounds can never be aware of themselves. Only awareness is aware of sound. I'll give you another example," he added.

"Think of the landscapes you create in your mind every night when you dream. Your dreams are populated with people who think and talk, as well as any number of inanimate objects, all equal projections within your mind, made up only of consciousness. The same applies to this universe we take to be real, but this universe is God's dream."

I thought about what he was saying. Although I under-stood, I remained unconvinced.

"Father, is there any way to prove God's existence?" I challenged.

"My child, God is the creator of science, so science can never prove God. Science can never master the Lord. And as I just said, God dwells within you as your own innate awareness of being. In the quiet depths of your heart, God is experienced as love, bliss, and unsurpassed peace. The only thing that separates you from the Lord is the never-ending stream of thoughts which cover your mind like a thick veil. If you want to experience God in a direct way, then all you need to do is to still your mind. The moment you do that, you'll realize your own divinity in a tangible way."

"Just still my mind," I replied. "Nothing more."

"Nothing more," he said. "That's why the Book of Psalms says, 'Be still and know that I am God.' It's like storm clouds obscuring the sun. The clouds never affect the sun, though they obstruct our vision. But the moment they clear away, the sun becomes visible in all its glory. But it's not so easy to still your mind," he added.

All of a sudden, I remembered my blood test and glanced at my watch. Ten minutes to go. I had to rush.

I stood up from my chair, feeling dizzy. "Father, I'm sorry to interrupt, but I have an appointment I must get to. I apologize for troubling you with impossible questions, but you did well," I added in a cavalier tone.

"My child, you still haven't confessed your sins," he whispered.

I smirked in the darkness, forgetting why I had stepped into the confessional in the first place. "Perhaps one day," I replied.

As I was about to open the door, I heard his voice again. "There's no reason for you to carry on with so much anger inside you."

I stopped dead in my tracks. "What was that?"

"All of that anger. I can help you overcome it while there's still time."

I stood for a moment, stunned by what I'd just heard. Was I in a psychologist's office or in a confessional with a priest? And what kind of priest gave lessons in metaphysics? I glanced over my shoulder at the black lattice that separated us, but I was unable to see his face. What did he know of my anger or my pain, and what on earth did he mean by "while there's still time?" Irritated, I stepped out of the penitent's booth and walked away without whispering a word.

15

THE CHILLS

$\mathcal{M}$y blood test proved fine, and by Saturday I felt normal again. Too bad I only had the weekend left before I had to report for my second round of chemo.

That night, the three of us treated ourselves to a fancy Japanese teppanyaki dinner. Claire had never seen an onion volcano before. She almost jumped out of her chair when the chef dropped his match onto the brandy, creating a firestorm in front of us.

I noticed Claire was warming up to me since her initial reaction to my diagnosis. She acted gracious and began listening when I spoke instead of letting her eyes drift away into some private world.

"Claire," I asked, "how does it feel to rule the school now that you're a senior?"

She rolled her eyes and smiled. "I can't wait to get the hell out of there."

"Why? Enjoy it while it lasts. Real life is just around the corner."

"Maybe," she said. "But if you had to deal with the idiots in my class, I don't think you'd say that."

I smiled, thinking of all of the characters I had known in high school, wishing for a moment to go back to the time when I roamed the hallways with my big round glasses and my biology textbook pressed against my chest.

~

We were shown to our new room at Mass General, and I was relieved to see that they had provided a proper cot where Anthony could sleep. I made a mental note to always insist on one from now on.

At around 1:00 p.m., the chemo and immunotherapies resumed their drip into my bloodstream. By early evening, I began to suffer from a terrible bout of chills, so I was put on the usual rotations of Demerol and Tylenol. But unlike my first cycle, when I had felt relatively good for the first three days, I already felt drained and exhausted.

As before, I slept during most of the week, getting up only to use the toilet, to walk, or to shove a few spoonfuls of food into my mouth. My nausea, aches, itching, and fevered chills were far worse than before, and, at one point, I broke down in tears because I doubted whether I would be able to push through it. I remember more than once just wishing that I could die.

On Friday afternoon, I caught a break from my nausea and decided to try to eat the food that my close friend Jill had cooked. As I savored her tomato rice, I realized that Dr. Connor was probably delivering my paper at the annual meeting in Philadelphia.

I reached for my phone and shot him an email, wishing him well and asking for an update. Half an hour later, I vomited whatever rice I had managed to eat right on the floor next to the bed. They cleaned me up and gave me another round of painkillers because I was shaking so violently, and in no time I was out like a light. In the early hours, my blood pressure dropped so low that I had to be awakened to receive oxygen.

16

CLUMPS IN MY HANDS

I felt as miserable as ever for about a week after I
finished my chemo cycle. I didn't have any strength
in my muscles, and my skin itched and burned as if I had been
stung by a jellyfish.

I knew that from now on things would get harder and
harder. With every new bag of chemo, my body would grow
weaker and weaker to the point where a blood transfusion
would become inevitable. While showering that night, clumps
of hair fell into my hands as I massaged shampoo into my
scalp. Although I always knew it was coming, the sight of my
hair limp over my fingers made my heart sink and brought
tears to my eyes.

After drying myself, I sat on a chair in the middle of the
bathroom while Anthony took an electric shaver to my head. I
rubbed some talcum powder onto my now shiny scalp and tied
a white and red handkerchief over it, making me look like some
kind of biker chick.

The loss of my hair, to my surprise, caused me to become
much more reactive and short-tempered. One night, as I lay
suffering in bed, Claire decided to blast her computer speakers.

"Lower that goddamn music!" I yelled at the top of my lungs.

"Hey, calm down," said Anthony.

I groaned something mean as I rolled onto my side about the pains of living with a stupid girl. As I drifted into sleep, I heard Anthony whisper, "She's my daughter, you know."

I felt better midway into my second week, except Claire hadn't forgotten my outburst. She made a show of it by sulking around the house. The loss of my hair also repulsed her on some level, so she went back to ignoring me as much as she could.

Between bouts of sleep, I tried to stay in touch with my colleagues at work by asking them to email me the latest trial data, though they told me to forget everything and focus on getting through my chemo.

Frustrated, I closed my laptop and pressed my head into the sofa.

With Claire at school and Anthony still at the office, the house was blissfully quiet. As I sat enjoying the silence, my mind drifted back to the priest and the last thing he had said to me. And though I was upset at the time, I couldn't help but admit that his comment had unearthed a great deal of anger and sorrow within me, which now felt like a twisted knot deep inside my chest.

I kept thinking of his offer to help me, although exactly what kind of help a Catholic priest could offer was beyond me. So, in the spur of the moment, I decided to leave some room before my next blood test to pay him another visit.

THE SECOND VISIT

*W*hen I stepped into the church I was enveloped by the same calm that I had sensed before, except, this time, three other people were praying in the pews. As I glanced at the confessional, I noticed the green light was already lit.

I let myself into the booth and sat on the chair.

"May the Lord who resides in your heart guide you to a good confession."

"Father, it's me, the doctor. We spoke a few weeks ago and—"

"Yes. I have not forgotten you."

"Can I trouble you for a little more of your time?" I whispered.

"If you wish," he replied.

"I've come back because last time you said something that stuck in my mind. You said that you could help me while there's still time, and I'd like to know what you meant by that."

He spoke after a long silence.

"Child, our time on this earth is uncertain. We never know

when it will end, but we all know sooner or later we're going to die."

"Yes."

"So time is precious. Every moment is precious."

As soon as he said that, I regretted coming back to the church.

"So you weren't referring to me specifically, you were just speaking about time in general?"

Another long silence, but, this time, he didn't respond.

"You also mentioned something about anger."

"Well, by the sound of your voice, it's plain to hear you're dragging around an awful amount of anger. Anger that you'd be wise to let go," he said.

I felt like a fool, since his warning, which had sounded so personal, was probably a stock phrase he used with everyone to catch their attention. I closed my eyes for a second, wondering if I should get up and leave.

"Anger is a double-edged knife," he said. "You cut yourself even as you inflict harm on others. It's a poison that consumes you," he added. "When you're angry, you're its first victim. We should—"

"Anger can be good," I interrupted, not in the slightest mood to listen to another lecture. "I dare to say it's given me the focus and motivation to get where I am today."

"And where are you today?"

"My daughter was three when she died from cancer," I said bluntly. "The senselessness of her loss so consumed me that I vowed to become a doctor so her death wouldn't be in vain."

"I'll pray for your loss," he replied. "May the Lord have mercy on her soul."

I sat in silence, letting his prayer fill my heart.

"Now," he continued, "no matter how much you think your pain shaped you into the person you are today, it wasn't without a heavy price. All victories are made hollow and empty with anger. It's like winning the battle but losing the war."

Great, I thought to myself. He's speaking in clichés.

"I disagree," I said. "I don't think the efforts I've made are either empty or hollow. In fact, they feel like a great triumph."

"Well, on the surface they might, but ask yourself if what you've achieved through anger has brought you any peace. How could it, when anger is the opposite of peace?"

I lowered my gaze, knowing there was truth to what he was saying. And yet, if my anger had indirectly saved a child's life, it was worth it even if it held me trapped in some kind of endless struggle. In that moment, I came to the realization that whatever peace I had enjoyed in life had left the day that Elaine died. I understood that the priest wasn't telling me that becoming a doctor wasn't worthy of respect. He was saying that living life through anger defeats the very purpose of life.

"Like a dam which prevents a great torrent of water from rushing forth," he continued, "sometimes anger is used as a wall to hold back deep pain and suffering. But if that anger prevents you from releasing your pain, it will destroy you in the end."

Of course, none of what he was telling me was new. I had heard it all before in one form or another. But I admit that what he said made me aware of how much anger I carried inside.

His voice softened. "If you can get through life by holding on to a minimum amount of anger and regret, you'll have so much more energy to get things done. Don't forget, anger robs you of all your joy. It stops you from giving and receiving love, and without love, life becomes a living hell. Just think of what this world would be like if people could let go of even a small part of their anger."

As I listened, I felt his words stir me from deep within, and my age-old cynicism began to loosen. I thought about my life, and I wondered if my own anger was preventing me from connecting with Claire or causing me to take Anthony's kindness for granted.

"Remember that your natural state is one of peace and contentment because God is the embodiment of peace," he said. "Anger takes you far away from the Lord."

"If anger is so harmful, why is it so common?" I asked, ignoring his reference to God.

"Anger rises when your desire to be in control is frustrated," he began. "You can read all the books you want, but you'll only be able to accept things for what they are when you understand that God is in control."

There was God again, always infiltrating every aspect of his talk. Needless to say, I had to expect it coming from a priest.

"Why should I accept things for what they are?" I challenged back. "There are plenty of things in this world that we should fight to change. Look at all of the children dying from leukemia we've managed to save. Should we have just prayed to God for help and done nothing? With all due respect, I wonder how many would still be alive today."

The priest sighed. "God has allowed leukemia to exist, as well as its cure. It's all part of the dance of creation. But surrender, which is what I'm referring to, doesn't mean refusing to act with the tools God has given you."

"So what does it mean?"

"Come back next week, and I'll tell you," he said. "I believe you need to be somewhere."

I had forgotten about the time again. I glanced at my watch, relieved to see I still had a few minutes left before my appointment. "I'd like to," I said.

"Father," I added, "there's something else I need to tell you."

"Yes, my child?"

"The truth is that if you could see me face-to-face, you'd

know that I'm also suffering from cancer. I'm actually a stage four patient."

"Then I will pray for you," he said in a solemn voice.

After a moment of silence, he added, "I can only imagine what it must be like to have lived through your daughter's cancer, only now to be faced with your own. May the Lord bless you and give you the strength to face your trials."

To my surprise, I made the sign of the cross and whispered, "Amen" under my breath.

18

HOLDING STEADY

*I*t turned out that my platelet and white blood cell count were critically low, but Dr. Yoshimura decided against a blood transfusion, at least for the time being. At home, Claire's ego had recovered, and she was talking to me again as if nothing had happened.

"Nice flats," she exclaimed as she walked past me.

Anthony sat in his study typing away on his laptop. He looked glum.

"What's wrong?" I asked.

He rubbed his forehead. "The bank sent me an email threatening to remove my line of credit."

Anthony stayed up late that night putting together a new business plan which detailed how he would stem his losses. He specifically laid out plans to open up new markets in Canada and Mexico, while keeping all of his products made in the U.S.A., which mattered to him. A trip to Toronto was already in the works, as soon as I was done with my chemo.

In the morning, Anthony stood before the hallway mirror fidgeting with his tie. "Without that line of credit, I'm toast," he said. "We won't last another six months."

"Tell them you need more time because you're seeing me through chemotherapy," I suggested. "Play the sympathy card," I said as he swallowed the last of his coffee before rushing out the door.

When he got back from his meeting, he looked pale and exhausted.

"Three months!" he exclaimed. "That's all I'm getting. Three damn months before they pull the plug."

I was back at the hospital a few days later for another CAT scan. Thankfully, no new tumors were detected, though the existing ones had failed to shrink.

"You have every reason to be optimistic," Dr. Yoshimura said with his characteristic smile. "The fact that your tumors are holding steady and haven't grown is a sign you're responding to the treatment."

If I were a layperson, I would have been happy to accept what he was telling me. But as a cancer doctor, I knew progress only exists when tumors shrink or disappear altogether. The body cannot survive for long with tumors that "hold steady." If they don't shrink, they are bound to grow larger. Since I didn't want to be rude, I nodded and smiled back while telling myself that I still had three chemo cycles left to go.

On Monday, my treatment started earlier than usual, and by noon I rolled with nausea and chills. I broke into a fever so high on the second night, it took the focused effort of three people to bring it down. By the third day, my skin erupted in painful small boils, and a large bruise developed on my right thigh. My nurse applied warm compresses over my body for hours on end, which did much to ease my pain. Yet despite her efforts, I woke up the following morning feeling helpless about my situation. With the itching, burning, and nausea bearing down on me from all sides, I finally succumbed to what I had seen other patients go through: a full-blown anxiety attack. It was as if a switch had flipped in my mind, making me acutely aware of how fragile I had become, while the never-ending waves of pain were like shackles I couldn't break free from. I hyperventilated so much that Anthony had to yell for a doctor, who gave me something strong to calm me down.

I cried tears of relief when recovery day arrived. I had survived the week, but not without consequence, since the chemo had caused me to pack on almost twenty pounds. My legs and feet had swollen as a side effect of the drip, so medication was prescribed to vacate the extra fluids in my body. When I stood up to walk down the hall, my feet felt puffy and swollen as if they had been replaced with elephant stumps. But I forced myself to walk anyway. On Sunday, after checking my vitals one last time, I was given the "all clear" to go home.

Back in the house, the atmosphere was tense but unusually quiet. Claire had been spending a lot of time with Danielle rehearsing their parts in *Pride and Prejudice*, which their drama class was putting on. This allowed Anthony and me the unusual luxury of enjoying a lot of alone time. It would have been wonderful, except for the fact that he was so stressed from work it made it impossible for him to relax. Instead of having the freedom to vent and cry on his shoulder, I felt obliged to keep my thoughts to myself. I sighed, frustrated from bouncing from one crisis to the next, which only added to my exhaustion.

To make matters worse, I revealed nothing of what was going on when my mother called again. Hiding the truth made me feel terrible, but I wanted to see how my chemotherapy turned out before dropping such a bombshell. Still, I ached for a sympathetic ear from someone whose feelings I didn't have to worry about. So by the time Thursday came around, I was ready to escape everything and spend some time with the priest.

19

THE THIRD VISIT

"May our Lord Jesus Christ bless you and keep you," said the priest as soon as I took my seat.

"Thank you, Father," I said. "If you recall, you were going to talk about surrender."

"Yes, my child. Surrender to God is the only way out of anger.

"The constant feeling," he began, "that we are always struggling against the current of life can be overcome. It's not something you have to live with."

"What is surrender?"

"There are many levels of surrender. At its most basic level, surrender is telling yourself whatever happens is for the best. You try to find the hidden lessons in life which make you stronger."

"Rolling with the punches," I threw in. "Or making lemonade out of lemons."

"Yes, but that's only a first step. At a deeper level, surrender is not trying to find meaning in every little thing that happens. It's simply refusing to brood over the past or worry about the future since the present moment is all there really is. It's as simple as letting go of all expectations and embracing this very moment for what it is."

"So we're back to accepting things as they are."

"Unconditionally accepting things as they are, which is a step further. But it's almost impossible to do, since the mind is obsessed with the past and future, in particular with regretting the past, complaining about the present, and trying to control the future."

"I can attest to that," I said. "But isn't our need to shape our future natural to our survival? Isn't it the very thing which makes us human? Our ability to think ahead and guide our destiny?"

"My child, God knows the past, present, and future. He knows what has been written for you, what the purpose of your life is, even what choices you will make. Nothing is hidden from God's sight. Knowing this, if you let the Lord carry your burden, placing all your joys and sorrows at His feet—holding nothing back—He will guide you. He will accomplish everything, for there is no end to His mercies."

I thought about what he was saying, but I just couldn't connect with the concept of God.

"If you can understand that God's will is behind everything, you can begin to step back and let go, inviting peace into your life. You'll begin to notice that in this world nothing lasts forever, everything changes. Day turns to night and night to day, rain to sunshine, and so forth. Sometimes we feel happy, other times sad. Pain is followed by pleasure, which is followed by more pain. The moon waxes and wanes. Everything in creation follows the same pattern. To know this while trying to make life conform to some fixed ideal of happiness is the height of ignorance."

"So the secret to happiness is to accept things as they are."

"Yes, and to understand that everything is transient. Acceptance not only takes care of our anger, it also leads us into joy and contentment. But for true acceptance, you must surrender your life to God. Trying to accept things blindly without understanding God's power is just another form of ignorance. It doesn't last. Sooner or later, you'll try to control everything again. And when you fail to get the results you want, you'll start resisting and complaining until it becomes your normal state of mind. But once you realize God is in control, it becomes possible to lay down your struggles at His feet.

"Surrender is the only way to peace," he repeated. "We have the choice in life to stand quietly on the banks of a raging river watching it flow by or to struggle against the current and get dragged into greater suffering."

"I don't know how I could ever surrender to the fact that I have cancer," I said.

"It doesn't mean that you shouldn't try to fight it. But you should accept that cancer is unfolding in your life right now, and be at peace with it. There's no point in resisting what is. You'll just waste precious energy that could be better spent fighting your disease."

"But isn't fighting cancer the opposite of accepting it?"

"No. You accept that you have cancer right now, leaving all your anger behind and taking refuge in Christ. Then you fight it with all your strength, while knowing the outcome is not in your hands but in God's hands."

"How can I be at peace with something so terrible? With something that might kill me?"

"You cannot find peace until you have firm faith in God. Faith that whatever is happening is written in your destiny and that His will prevails. Remember, not even a leaf can fall from a tree if God doesn't allow it to happen. Only after you grasp this can divine peace be yours."

My thoughts turned to all of the horrible things that go on in this world.

"If God is in control, if God is all-powerful, why is there so much evil in this world? How can He allow such terrible things to happen?"

I listened while the priest took a deep breath as if preparing to deliver a long sermon.

"Child of God, I should not have to remind you that all of the Lord's acts are just and good. He is not responsible for a single act of evil we see in this fallen world."

"But you just said that nothing happens unless he allows it to happen. Now you're saying he isn't responsible for any evil. This kind of glaring contradiction is one of the reasons I refuse to believe in God," I said, my voice trembling.

"Your position is understandable," he said to my surprise. "It's not easy reconciling the darkness in this world with God's light."

"I say it proves there's no God, or, if there is a God, it's not one I would care to worship."

"To understand how God is just," he began, ignoring what I had just said, "you first need to understand a few of His spiritual laws. You have to see things from the point of view of a person standing at the top of a hill who is able to look down at an expanse of city, seeing how all of the streets and buildings connect. We, on the other hand, are like a person standing in the middle of a street whose view is obstructed by high walls."

"I'm not following."

"God has set down many laws. One of them, no doubt, is the law of free will. But God has also ruled that one will reap what they sow. In other words, we have no choice except to experience the consequences of our actions."

"That sounds nice," I said. "I understand how cause and effect works, but I don't see how it has anything to do with the evil that surrounds us. What about all of the innocent people who are murdered every day or the countless children who come to harm from no fault of their own? Are they responsible for what happened to them? And what about those who get away with murder and die quietly of old age?"

"Yes, on the face of things God's law doesn't appear to work very well, but that's because you're observing things from within a small segment of time. You're not seeing the big picture."

"How so?"

"I've said before that the soul is eternal. And what is the soul, but a conditioned form of God's light? And light is a vibration of energy, of consciousness. Even a physicist as renowned as Albert Einstein declared that energy can neither be created nor destroyed, only changed in form."

"He was referring to physical forms of energy."

"It also applies to subtle forms of energy, like the human mind and the soul. Our soul, which is the body of the mind, lives on after death. It does not perish. Because the soul is a form of energy which is indestructible and destined for eternal life, it must submit to God's law and experience the fruits of all the actions it has ever committed. But for that to transpire, the soul must return to this world again and again."

I sat in silence for a few seconds, trying to process what the priest was suggesting.

"Pardon me, but are you talking about reincarnation? I don't recall seeing it in the Bible or learning about it in Sunday school."

The priest laughed. "With the Lord as my witness, know that I would never utter a word which is contrary to our scripture. But what the Bible hints at is not always obvious even though the truth is there."

"Like what?"

"In the Book of Revelation, John says, 'He who overcomes, I will make him a pillar in the temple of My God, and he will not go out from it anymore.' The word anymore hints at the soul's movement from earth to heaven and back again."

"I'm sorry, but isn't it a stretch to believe in reincarnation based on a single word?" I asked.

"There's much more," the priest continued. "In the Gospel of Matthew, Jesus is asked about Elijah coming before the Messiah. Jesus himself makes it clear that Elijah had already come and that he was John the Baptist. In other words, Jesus confirms that John the Baptist was the reincarnation of the prophet Elijah."

"Well, I don't know the gospels like you do, but is it possible you're just misinterpreting the Bible?"

"No. There's simply no other way to read that passage. The hints are all around us. Consider a pebble, dropped in a puddle of water. Ripples extend out and return until the puddle is still and mirrorlike. Energy always seeks to harmonize itself into a state of rest. The same applies to actions. The saying 'what goes around, comes around' is more accurate than people realize. Our bodies, minds, thoughts and actions, everything—these are nothing except God's light, which always seeks to return to a state of quiescence.

"Look around," he continued, "and tell me if there can be any other explanation for the suffering of innocent people? To say otherwise reduces God to a cruel arbitrary dispenser of fate."

"Frankly," I snapped back, "I find it offensive to suggest that the millions of men, women, and children who were sent to the gas chambers during the Holocaust deserved what they got. If people are taught to believe that every time they suffer a misfortune they're getting what they deserve, they'll just feel guilty or bad about themselves all the time."

"On the contrary, there's nothing to feel guilty about once you're armed with correct understanding. The knowledge that misfortune is God's way of releasing us from past wrongs allows us to accept the blows that life gives us with serenity. If we can understand that there are lifetimes of actions which must be accounted for, both good and bad, the apparent chaos and randomness of life begins to make sense."

"How does God judge whether an action is good or bad? What is seen as good in some cultures is considered terrible in others."

"That's an important point. It's not the action itself which determines the result, but the intention behind the action. A surgeon cuts into a body with a scalpel, but the intention is the opposite of a murderer who kills with a knife. Deep in their heart, a person knows whether an action is helpful or harmful, selfless or selfish, honest or deceitful."

"So all the people who marched to their deaths in Auschwitz were guilty of some prior sin from some other lifetime which must have been so terrible as to cause them to deserve such a fate?"

"I know it is painful to accept. But if it were otherwise, how could God be just? How could God be merciful if He were to allow someone to suffer without proper justification?"

"So much for mercy," I quipped.

"Listen, God does not bring suffering on anyone. His natural law dispenses suffering to relieve those who, by their own deeds, have brought suffering to others. Removing that burden is an act of mercy. Otherwise, people would be able to do whatever they wanted to without any accountability, which would make a mockery of God."

"Even children?"

"Yes, even children, if you consider their storehouse of good and bad actions spans many lifetimes."

I shook my head in disbelief, staring at the black lattice which divided us. Through its diamond-shaped openings I could see the priest's pale ear as it moved through the shadows.

"Don't you think if we believe people deserve what they get, then we'll stop caring about them when they're suffering?"

"It's not that they deserve what they get, in the sense of a parent punishing a child to teach him a lesson. It's simply that God's law is impartial and unrelenting. Good actions lead to good effects and vice versa, and the slate must be cleaned again and again. That impartiality is what makes God just. In fact, from the highest perspective, God does not punish or reward anyone. We are the architects of our own fate. That's the beauty of free will, and it's the reason why God is not responsible for any of the evils in this world. We just have to grasp the vast timelines involved to make sense of why things happen to us."

"But you still haven't answered my question. What about caring for others?"

"Paul teaches in Galatians, 'Do not be deceived: God is not mocked, for whatever one sows, that will he also reap.' Accepting the truth of 'what we sow so shall we reap' does nothing to reduce our empathy for others. People have no memories of their past lives. When we see misfortune befall a good person, we suffer along with them knowing they are inno-cent in this life, so to speak, even if we understand that what is happening is just in God's eyes."

"But God won't stop it?"

"God is all-powerful and can start or stop anything He wants. That's why we never turn away from God but always pray for His mercy. Although we must also learn to accept God's laws."

"If reincarnation is true, why don't we have any memory of our past lives?"

The priest cleared his throat. "It's another mercy from God that we're not able to remember our past lives. If we were able to see all of the things we have done, all of the people we have loved, all of the people we have hurt, and all of the people we have been, we would become overwhelmed, saddened, and confused. We wouldn't be able to relate to those in our present lives. Just consider how much suffering arises only from the traumas lived in this life. So not remembering all of the pain that we have given and received is in itself a great blessing.

"Some things are okay to forget," he added. "There is healing in forgetting."

"If we are reborn again and again," I said, "where does that leave eternal heaven and eternal damnation?"

"Only God is eternal. Even his heavens and hells cannot escape the jaws of time, however many eons they last. Remember, whatever has been created is transient, including all of the worlds of light and darkness that have sprung from the Lord's Word."

"Are you saying there is more than one heaven?"

The priest chuckled. "I find it amusing that in this world, which is so varied with millions of species, plants, and landscapes, people believe that God would limit his creation to a uniform white cloudy space for all souls to congregate."

"So how many heavens are there?"

"As many as God desires, for time, space, and dimension are no obstacle. There are many heavens and hells, and the soul is sent to a corresponding plane which reflects the moral life it lived. But even the worst offenders, who are burning in the hottest fires or freezing in the coldest ice, will eventually return to this world to experience the fruits of their past actions. Likewise, those who for ages have enjoyed the pleasures of heaven will become compelled to enter into another womb to continue to reap the rewards of their good actions."

"So when does it all end?"

"It ends when the soul merges back into the expanse of God's being, like a wave returning to the ocean or a thought dissolving back into silence."

"And when does that happen?"

"It happens when you realize you are not just a human body and mind, but are in essence the eternal awareness we call God. 'Be still and know that I am God' can also be understood as 'Still your mind and know that you are one with God.' Then the dream of life and creation ends for that soul."

All of this talk of suffering and death caused Elaine to enter my mind. "Father, why did my daughter have to die so young? According to you, she was responsible for her own fate."

"She did nothing wrong, my child. Take comfort in knowing the moment of death is set at birth, and the moment of the next birth is set at death. We cannot know why a person's lifetime is written in days or years. There are many factors involved. Some of it has to do with the purpose of the work that needs to be accomplished, for every child touches the world and the people around her. Sometimes unresolved relationships carry over to the next life and last only a few years until they are settled, and some of it has to do with the spiritual lessons souls are able to receive only after they are dragged through the depths of grief."

"But I thought you said that everything happens to us as a result of our own past actions? Did I do something in the past that would cause her to die young?"

"Of course not. Although each soul has its own destiny, our destinies intertwine in mutual fulfillment. Most of our lives are spent by creating new actions while experiencing the fruits of past actions in a never-ending cycle which can only be broken through spiritual emancipation. But some of what happens in life is not a direct consequence of our past actions, but a nudge from the Lord who resides in our hearts so we may turn our minds in His direction. For better or for worse, suffering is an effective tool to help us awaken from the dream of life."

"So Elaine had to die for my own spiritual growth?"

"My child, I know you are suffering. But that doesn't mean you need to sling mud at the Lord. Of course, your daughter was not sacrificed for your spiritual growth. What kind of God would behave so callously? Your daughter's three years were already written in her book of life even before she was born, and you had nothing to do with it. Sometimes a person is visited by a terrible illness for no other reason than the time has come for that soul to release from the body. In such cases, they're not meant to glean spiritual lessons, but just move on."

"Is that what happened to Elaine?" I asked.

"I would like to think so," he replied.

"Does every illness contain some kind of spiritual teaching?"

"No. Physical illness is a natural part of having a body. The fact the body gets sick is a reminder to the soul that the body is not who we really are, because the soul is not subject to decay. In this way, it might be said that illness contains a hidden spiritual lesson. Yet getting sick doesn't necessarily mean we're experiencing the fruits of a past action, though it may well be the case.

"As for you," he continued, "it just so happened that your daughter was born of your womb because God ruled you needed to experience terrible grief so you could turn your mind to higher things. He matched her short life with yours so you could grow from her death. Your lives were parallel tracks which joined for a brief moment in time before separating again. Yet your daughter did not die for the sake of your spiritual growth. Had she been born to another mother, I do not believe her fate would have been any different. But God appointed you as her mother so you could grow spiritually from what was already fated to occur."

I tried to speak, but he interrupted me.

"Don't try to second-guess the Lord on His plan, for it's beyond our capacity to understand how God is able to orchestrate all the moving pieces of creation into a unified tapestry which serves His purpose. What matters is that you surrender to Him, for everything happens according to His will through the laws which He has set down. Only then will you feel sheltered by His presence. Only then will you be able to experience real peace. Only then will you be able to rid yourself of your anger. But you must guard against trying too hard to understand why this or that happened since we are not endowed with divine vision."

After a moment of silence, he said, "I've taken the time to explain all of this so you can begin to let go and feel a little of the peace and love which flows eternally from the Lord."

The mention of time caused me to sit up straight. Even before I looked at my watch, I knew I was late.

"Before you go," he said, "if you doubt that these teachings come from the Bible, let me leave you with what the prophet Isaiah said, 'Tell the righteous it shall be well with them, for they shall eat the fruit of their deeds. Woe to the wicked, it shall be ill with him, for what his hands have done shall be done to him.'

"Contemplate it," he said, "and I think you'll find the meaning crystal clear."

O

ON PINS AND NEEDLES

*T*o my disappointment, my fourth cycle of biochemotherapy didn't start well. While I was having my catheter inserted, I broke into a serious nosebleed. After the nurses stemmed the bleeding, the doctors ran the usual tests and, for some reason, everything had dropped. My hemoglobin, platelets, and white blood cells were all down, though still hovering just above the limit for my chemo to continue. That explained the nosebleed and why I had felt so exhausted over the weekend.

As I sat in my hospital bed, waiting for another nurse to arrive, I kept hearing the priest's words playing in my mind. Especially his points on reincarnation. To kill time, I allowed myself to fantasize about whether Elaine was enjoying some beautiful heaven suitable to a three-year-old, or whether her soul had already been reborn. But the more I thought about it, the more questions came to mind, such as whether Elaine's soul had retained its form as a child or whether it had reverted into a more adult version of herself since she had presumably already lived many lives. If reincarnation was real, why was the world's population always increasing, and where did the extra souls come from?

The slam of a metal drawer at the nurse's station jolted me back to reality, and I laughed at myself for dwelling on things I didn't even believe in.

As the drugs dripped into my body, I slipped into an uncomfortable daze I'd never felt before. I grew lightheaded and, within two hours, suffered from severe stomach cramps. I made an effort to eat the mashed potatoes and boiled vegetables on my dinner tray, but only managed to take a few bites before falling asleep.

Around 3:00 a.m., I woke up with chest pains and to the beeping sound of my heart monitor. In a few seconds, the pain crawled up to my neck and spread over my left temple. A ripple of pins and needles fanned out over my chest and upper back. When my left arm started to tingle, I was certain I was in the middle of a heart attack. By then the doctors and nurses were all around me, trying to get a handle on the situation. All of a sudden, my face and chest started burning as if they were on fire, and I could feel my heart pounding at what felt like three times its normal speed.

It turned out I was suffering a heart arrhythmia, and a quick shot of a calcium channel blocker was all it took to get my heart rate back to normal. After my dizziness subsided, Anthony held my hand and told me that he thought he was going to lose me because I had turned so pale.

The rest of the week passed without any other major incidents. I again grew bloated and suffered intense nausea and stomach cramps and slept as much as I could. I no longer cared how many days went by before I was able to shower, or how little I managed to get out of bed to walk up and down the hallway. I just wanted to sleep until the chemo had run its course.

When my discharge day arrived, Anthony had to carry me to the car. Since my blood numbers were so low, Dr. Yoshimura asked me to return for more tests in forty-eight hours. His instincts proved right when I awoke the following morning to a bloodstained bedsheet. I had suffered another major nosebleed but had been so out of it that it had failed to rouse me.

A few hours after my blood tests, Dr. Yoshimura stepped into the waiting room with a frown.

"Your platelets, white blood cells, and your hemoglobin are all at rock bottom."

"How soon can we transfuse?" I asked, knowing exactly what was coming.

"I'm setting it up as we speak," he replied.

I felt a lot better in the days after my transfusion, although I mostly slept. I kept worrying about whether the foreign blood in me had been properly screened, until I realized how point-less it was to stress about such things relative to the cancer attacking me.

Anthony was in a better mood since the bank had thrown him a lifeline, and Claire was also going through a good phase. We knew her drama class had lifted her spirits, although I wondered about all of her other homework.

I didn't see much of Claire, though, since I was bedridden. Breakfast, lunch, and dinner were all brought to my room. Anthony even set up a new flat-screen television on our dresser so I could catch up on some of my favorite shows. Still, I never found the energy to watch for more than twenty minutes at a time.

I was scheduled for another set of CAT scans during the second week of my recovery. As we drove to the hospital, I real-ized I was a nervous wreck. After putting up with so much agony from the chemotherapy, I couldn't bear to hear even a single piece of bad news. I was terrified to receive the same heartbreaking results I sometimes had to deliver to the hope-filled parents of my young patients.

After spending half a day at the hospital, we drove back the next morning to meet with Dr. Yoshimura. When he walked into the room, he beamed from ear to ear.

"The news couldn't be better," he said. "Your tumors have shrunk dramatically."

"Which ones, and by how much?" the doctor in me asked.

"All of them, and by over fifty percent. The only one showing resistance is the cancer in your thyroid."

Fifty percent shrinkage with no new growths was indeed miraculous. It meant that Dr. Yoshimura had chosen the right combination of chemo and immunotherapy drugs. I turned to Anthony and burst into tears.

Dr. Yoshimura passed me a tissue.

"Laura," he said, "your response was so good, I'm thinking of adding a sixth cycle of chemo to your protocol if you can tolerate it," he said.

By "tolerate it" he meant whether my blood counts would remain high enough to manage the chemo without risk of internal bleeding or cardiac arrest.

"But my arrhythmia…" I said.

"Yes, it's a concern. But as you know, arrhythmia is a common reaction to the drugs. Your blood results will tell us how to proceed. If they drop again, we'll see about that sixth cycle."

I nodded, analyzing his words. I wasn't against adding another cycle with these results, but my attack of arrhythmia had really shaken me.

"What about my thyroid? When are you planning to operate?" I asked.

"It could happen anytime, depending on the lab results." Having surgery to remove my thyroid had always been part of the plan. It was just a question of when.

As we drove down Storrow Drive, I observed the backs of people who were sitting on benches by the Charles River, some alone, others with company, and I wondered about their lives. Were they happy? Lonely? In love?

Anthony put his hand on my knee, pulling me out of my daze. He said he wanted to take me out for a celebratory lunch, but, as much as I would have loved it, I was just too tired to sit through a meal.

Three days later, another blood test revealed that my platelets and white blood cells had again dropped significantly. All my excitement over my so-called progress went up in smoke.

All things considered, the decline was not unexpected. It was a side effect of the chemo and had nothing to do with the cancer.

"I'm sorry, but we'll have to postpone your next round of chemo until we stabilize your blood," Dr. Yoshimura said over the phone.

"What's next, then?"

"Another transfusion, I'm afraid."

21

THE FOURTH VISIT

A week after my second transfusion, I felt strong enough to drive myself to the hospital for my follow-up test, but I made sure to leave home early so I could swing by the church.

"May our Lord Jesus Christ bless you and keep you," said the priest's familiar voice.

"It's me again."

"What burdens your mind today, my child?"

"Father, I was thinking about what you said the other day. When Elaine died, if reincarnation exists, did she rise to heaven as a three-year-old or in some other form?"

"Must we know everything?" he whispered. "Is it not better to have faith in the Lord and His works?"

"So you don't know," I said.

"If you must know," he began, "I believe at death the body keeps the form in which it died. A child remains a child in its body of light until it reenters another womb. Many have witnessed the ghostly appearances of children or adults who at death have, for one reason or another, failed to cross into the light."

I was about to ask if Elaine had suffered the same fate when he read my mind.

"This doesn't mean your daughter got stuck between worlds," he said.

"What if a newborn dies? They're barely aware of their surroundings. Is there a heaven for newborns?"

"Such souls may enter another womb immediately after death, or they rest in a state of sleep until their time to be reborn arrives."

"Another question," I began. "If people are constantly dying and coming back, how is it that the world's population is always increasing?"

The priest let out his customary chuckle. "Do you have any idea how many souls dwell in the higher realms? How do you know they haven't existed for ages, even before this world of earth and water was breathed into being, and will continue to exist even after this world is burnt by the sun? You should think of this world as nothing more than a train station, with souls entering and exiting at all times. But the individuals you see on the platform do not reveal how many people populate the countries they come from."

"Interesting."

"Perhaps, but there's little point in dwelling on things that have no effect on our day-to-day lives," he added. "We can speculate about how the Lord designed His creations, but what good will it do us? Will it bring us any closer to Him? Will it grant us any peace?"

I agreed such talk was rather pointless. I thought of my illness and felt depressed.

"Father, my life was going well until recently. So why cancer? Why me? Why now? Even after I've suffered more than my fair share, I fear God wants to strike me down."

"It may feel that way, but sometimes suffering is really God's grace in disguise."

"Frankly, I've heard that excuse one time too many."

"Nonetheless, as long as you feel you are an individual who is separate from God, so long as you are without faith, as long as you are dazzled by the pleasures and promises of this fallen world, you are bound to suffer. And there can be no other way, for only wholeness in God brings peace and joy. Understand that being an individual is by definition the exact opposite of wholeness. You are separate, isolated. A fragile body of flesh and bones."

"But we are what we are," I protested. "Even if I wanted to, I can't change the fact that I'm a human being."

"That is true, but you can change your focus."

"In what way?"

"Instead of running after career, status, money, and comforts, hoping they'll bring you fulfillment, you need to turn your attention inward to the indwelling spirit. That's where true happiness lies. But not a soul in the world will do it simply because they are told to, so God has devised several ways to allow the soul to mature. The first is slow, allowing a person to enjoy and suffer the consequences of his own actions for a long time until he grows weary and questions whether there's something deeper and more rewarding than this fleeting show we call life.

"The second method is more painful, but faster, and it occurs when God sends unexpected forms of suffering to coax the soul to wake up from the false promises of this world."

"But I was happy with my life."

"Happiness is relative. In comparison to God's bliss, your so-called happiness is nothing but misery."

"But I was happy—"

"My child, God knows what's right for you," he interrupted. "His only wish is to redeem you. The pains and struggles your daughter led you through were not designed to strike you down. Your current suffering is not meant to destroy you.

On the contrary, everything was designed to elevate you. They're an opening to enable you to regain your lost faith."

"I've never had any faith."

"Every child is born with a natural faith in God until they are taught to believe otherwise."

Maybe he was right. I had to admit that I remembered praying to God as a young girl.

"Children are naturally close to the Lord since they've just returned from inhabiting a body of light," he said.

"But it seems cruel to impose suffering as a way to turn people to God."

"It's not the only way," he said. "Some rare souls wake up to the realization that this world is not their final home. They feel spontaneous devotion to God and begin to yearn for His presence. In time they reach a point where a Master appears who teaches them how to still their turbulent minds and let go of their worldly desires until they finally merge into the pure ocean of God-consciousness. But such souls are extremely rare. Most awaken to God through plain old suffering."

"So that's why I'm suffering like this? What if I die before I regain this faith in God you say I need?"

"It's not just faith. It's a deep yearning to return to God's side. Faith is only the first step, so do not make the mistake of thinking that everyone you see suffering will give themselves to Jesus in this lifetime. People will keep running after material things even though those things cheat them again and again. It takes a long time before a soul has experienced enough hardship for it to begin to finally lift its gaze to God."

"How long?"

"Every soul is different. But the Lord is not in any hurry, since the Lord is beyond time."

"Great. So my suffering continues."

"Your suffering is a blessing. It's an act of compassion, however difficult it may be to accept. From God's perspective, whatever causes you to suffer in life is nothing compared to the suffering of being blind to God's blissful presence. If you surrender to Him, all of your anguish will vanish in an instant."

I closed my eyes and tried to locate God within me. But I was only met by the darkness behind my eyelids, by fatigue, and by the aches and pains moving through my body.

22

A NEW LEAF

*D*r. Yoshimura gave the go-ahead to resume my chemo the day after my blood tests confirmed that my platelets had climbed to over one hundred. As the drugs flooded my system, bringing fever and chills, I welcomed the narcotic pain relievers that knocked me out for hours on end.

I didn't feel any better when I came around. When I tried to inhale through the spirometer, the instrument that measures lung capacity, the piston barely rose. I had zero strength in my lungs.

By morning, I was coughing badly and running a fever of 104 degrees. Chills upon chills rippled through me. I broke into a sweat so heavy they had to wrap me with towels. When the doctors ordered another round of blood tests and a chest x-ray, they had to wheel me away because I was too sick to walk.

By the time the lab results came back, it was clear I was in the throes of pneumonia. To fight the infection, they hooked me up to yet another IV line that fed me a cocktail of antibiotics. After forty-eight hours of hell, the sweats and coughing finally began to clear up. But I was so ill and nauseous from the immunotherapy, I just wanted to curl up into a ball and die.

It was while I was lying on my back, listening to nothing except the sound of my wheezing, when I heard a knock on the door. Anthony got up from his chair and pushed the privacy curtain aside.

"Dr. Connor," he whispered.

"Anthony. Good to see you."

I couldn't make out the rest of their conversation, but it was clear Anthony was getting all worked up.

"Yes, I'll give her the envelope as soon as she's better," was the last I heard him say before the room fell silent.

In the morning, on the fifth day of my cycle, Dr. Yoshimura suspended my chemotherapy. My blood levels had fallen too low to carry on, and I hadn't yet fully recovered from my pneumonia. Given the progress I had made, he decided it was just too risky for me to continue. Although I wasn't aware of it at the time, my difficult journey through chemotherapy had come to an abrupt end.

I was held in recovery for four days before I was allowed to go home. As always, I felt exhausted, and my skin seemed to peel more than usual. Ten days later, after I had forgotten about Dr. Connor's visit, Anthony placed a thick manila envelope on our bed. He opened it and leafed through a bound document almost one hundred pages long.

"What is it?" said Anthony.

"It's an amended trial protocol."

"I don't know what in the world he's thinking," Anthony said, raising his voice. "He has some nerve to ask anything of you while—"

"It must be important," I said, interrupting him.

"It better be."

I flipped through the pages and sighed. A handwritten letter was buried at the bottom.

Dear Laura,

I hope you are gaining ground with each passing day. You're terribly missed around here, and we're all counting on seeing you back. The annual meeting was a great success, and I am sorry you weren't able to bask in the credit you deserved. But onwards and upwards, I say, the greater prize is still at hand. On that note, I have taken the liberty to enclose the amended protocol that Michael and the rest have completed in your absence. I was hoping you could read through it and write a brief analysis, specifically on the study design and efficacy sections before we send it off. I want to make sure we're both on the same page. Take your time, of course, there's no rush. What matters is that you feel better. We're counting the days for you to be declared NED, so please don't delay in letting me know how you're coming along. If you need anything at all, remember you can reach me 24/7. Kind regards, Brendan.

Anthony took the letter from my hand and read it.

"He must be out of his mind."

"It's all right," I said with half-closed eyes. "It means I'm still in the game. Not yet forgotten."

"Of course you're not forgotten, but to ask you to work when you're not even a minute out of chemo makes no sense."

"Relax," I said. "It's not such a big deal. Actually, it's a good thing. I'm going to get back to work and publish in *The Lancet* exactly as planned." But despite my fighting words, deep down I knew I was the first person I was trying to convince.

❧

With my chemo over, Anthony and I sat with Dr. Yoshimura to map out the next phase of my treatment.

"After your thyroidectomy, I'll start you on another immunotherapy drug. If all goes well, I expect to see continued shrinkage of the tumors in your clavicular lymph node, lung, and ascending colon."

Continued shrinkage isn't the same as total elimination, I remarked to myself.

"What about a lymphadenectomy?" I asked.

"It's a possibility we'll consider after we assess your response to the treatment. If your response is good, and the tumors have shrunk like I hope they will, we can talk about removing the lymph nodes on the right side of your body."

Dr. Yoshimura stood to shake my hand before moving in for a quick hug.

"You're doing so well, Laura. Keep it up."

The surgery to remove my thyroid wouldn't move forward until Dr. Yoshimura confirmed that my blood levels had recovered. Claire was excited because one of her friends had found an off-season deal at a resort in Cancun, and she was pestering Anthony to let her travel on her own.

"You can party with your friends once you're in college," he told her.

That night, while we were lying in bed watching TV, I turned to him and said, "You deserve a break. Why don't you take her to a resort for a week?"

He shook his head. "What am I going to do all day sitting on a beach?"

"Then take her on a cruise," I suggested.

He thought about it for a second. "Oh, she'd love that, but I don't think it's the right time."

"Look," I said, resting my hand on his arm. "You've slept in that back-breaking cot for weeks, waking up at all hours of the night to—"

"I could chill in the casino while Claire runs around the ship," he said.

"Yes, you could relax. And don't worry about the money," I said. "I want you to take a break before my surgery."

"On second thought, forget it. My company is crumbling, you're going through the worst time of your life, and I'm supposed to go off on a boat on your dime? I don't think so."

I propped myself up against my pillows. "Yes, it sounds crazy, but sometimes we need to do crazy things to protect our sanity. I've never seen you so tired."

"I'm fine," he said.

"The truth is, this is not only about you. To be honest, I have a long road ahead, and it's better for both of us if you come back rested and recharged."

"How do you think my employees will feel, knowing their boss went off on a cruise while they are at risk of losing their jobs?"

"Tell them you took me to visit my mother. They don't have to know where you went."

"What about the cost?"

"Forget about the cost," I said. "I'm the one offering."

Anthony thought about it in silence. "If I go, who's going to look after you?"

"I'll ask Jill to spend the week with me if she can take time off. It'll be great."

He looked me straight in the eye. "On the subject of your mother, when are you going to tell her? It's just not right, you know."

"Soon," was all I could muster, though I didn't have a clue when I'd find the courage to tell her.

"Well, it better be soon," he added, "or I'll call her myself."

He was right. Keeping my mother in the dark was no longer an option.

23

THE FIFTH VISIT

*I*t took a little arm wrestling to convince him, but four days later Anthony and Claire flew out to Florida to catch their ship. They had chosen a tour around the Bahamas, St. Thomas, and St. Martin. When I reminded them to pile on the sunscreen, Claire made it clear she intended to come back with a nice tan.

"That's the perfect thing to say to a melanoma patient," I said, rolling my eyes.

We squabbled until Anthony stepped in, forcing her to apologize.

As soon as they were off, the house settled into an oasis of peace. Jill was busy in the kitchen cooking dinner while I sat on the sofa, watching another rerun of *Marley & Me*.

"I guess it'll take another three to four weeks for your hair to start growing back," she said.

"Looks like it."

Of all of the people I had met in medical school, Jill was one of the few friends I had stayed in touch with. After we graduated, she remained at Yale to specialize in ophthalmology before moving back to Boston to start up her practice.

As soon as we finished eating, she slipped back into the kitchen.

"I have a surprise for you," she said, gliding back to the family room with three different flavors of Häagen-Dazs ice cream: vanilla, pistachio, and dark chocolate.

"I'll have a bit of each," I said, smiling.

"That's my girl," she said.

"You know," she added, "I'm not here to help you with your chemo recovery. I'm here to help you with your chemo celebration."

"Jill, that's so sweet. But you know there's still cancer in my body."

"I know, but I also know you'll soon be NED. I can feel it. And your chemo is over, so there's no way in hell we're not going to celebrate."

"If you say so," I whispered.

It had been over a month since I last visited the priest. When I stepped into the church, I was reminded of why I always felt the need to come back. There was something special within those gray walls. Perhaps it was the light which flowed through the stained glass, or the high stone arches that offered protection from the outside world, or the welcoming scent of old wood. Whatever it was, there was something alluring about the place that made me want to sit and take it all in.

When Thursday came around, I told Jill a little white lie. I made it sound like I had completely forgotten that I needed to swing by the hospital for a follow-up weigh-in when, in fact, none was scheduled.

"I'll take you," she said.

"Oh, don't worry about it. You've been babysitting me

around the clock. Why don't you take a few hours for your-self?" I suggested.

"If you're sure, okay then. I'll drop by the supermarket to pick up a few things for tonight's cookathon."

"You're the best," I said, giving her a hug.

I lowered myself onto a pew and let my eyes rest on the large figure of Jesus on the cross. Though he was deeply wounded and in obvious pain, he still managed to radiate an unshakable peace. In the depths of my heart I also wished that I could feel some of that peace as I fought against my cancer.

As I sat there, lost to my thoughts, it occurred to me that I had been missing Anthony even though he had only been away for a few days. For a second, my eyes followed an old lady who was shuffling through the church until I noticed, as always, the green light bulb burning above the confessional.

"May our Lord Jesus Christ bless you and keep you."

"Good afternoon, Father."

"My child, how are you?"

"Better. I finished my chemo. Or rather, we took it as far as it could go. But there's still cancer in my body."

"I'm sorry to hear that."

"There are still other treatments to pursue, and I'm having surgery in a few days," I said, not sure why I was sharing such details.

"I will pray that your operation goes well," he said. "Now tell me, what's pulling on your heart strings today?"

"Tell me about love," I said out of the blue.

"Love?" he said. "Why, God is love, and love is God. Jesus is love, and you are love. Not much else needs to be said."

"Father, it sounds nice when you put it that way, but what do you mean when you say that I am love?"

"Love is not an emotion among many. It's much more sublime than that. It's the essence of your being."

"I've known what love feels like, but it's never a constant. Mind you, I loved my daughter, and I will always love her. But if I am love itself, as you put it, then why don't I feel it right now?"

"You don't feel it because you think love is something that happens when another person brings it out of you. Most people who are lonely lament that they have no one to love and are not loved. What they fail to realize is they are love itself."

"So why don't we feel it?"

"When you meet someone and fall in love, you project the love already in you onto that person, making you think they're the cause of your love. Later on, if you argue and fight, the love that was there seems to vanish, and you bemoan your condition. But in truth love neither comes nor goes. It's always there."

"If that's so, I still don't get why I don't feel it all the time."

"As long as you believe you are this body of flesh and blood, you'll need another body to project your love onto. But once you are able to quiet your mind and sense the oneness between you and God, you will immediately experience true love, which is free and independent of anything or anyone. Love is what you feel when you become aware of God, because God is nothing but love, and God is at the center of your being."

"Father, this is all highly idealistic. Even if I were to accept that the saints can bask in some kind of spiritual love, it's out of reach for the rest of us."

"Yes, you're right, but it doesn't mean you shouldn't strive to kindle that divine love in your heart. Love for Jesus is the purest kind of love. It's the love which both redeems and saves. When, through God's grace, you are able to love Jesus with all of your heart, you'll realize that love is not a mere feeling. Love is a state of being."

"Okay, but where does that leave the love between ordinary people? Between a husband and wife or a mother and child?"

The priest sighed. "I'm sorry to tell you, but most of the so-called love between people is just another business transaction. When expectations are attached to love, that love is tainted."

"So people shouldn't love one another?" I asked.

"Of course, everyone should strive to love, even if it's tainted by selfish motives. In fact, there's no choice because the soul is always searching for a way back to its natural state, just as a pendulum is always moving back to the center. The need to love and to be loved are reflections of our deeper divinity, though human love is mostly flawed."

What the priest said didn't apply to my love for Elaine, which was pure and unconditional, but it reminded me of all of my ups and downs with Jeremy. In the beginning, I couldn't take my eyes off him, and the qualities that had first attracted me to him were, in the end, the same ones that tore us apart. When it came to Anthony, I had to admit I no longer felt strong emotions, just a kind of constant warmth for him. The more I thought about it, the more I questioned how real or pure my love for Anthony was.

"Pure love always leads back to the Lord," he added, as if reading my mind. "Pure love is the bridge that allows us to make contact with God."

I lowered my head. "Well, for those of us with little or no faith, where does that leave us?"

"My child, if you want to feel more love, you should start by loving yourself. You should start by knowing your own true worth. You have been molded from God's breath, which makes you divine. What's the use in running around, praising other people, when you don't even know your own worth as a child of God?"

"But I thought we were all hopeless sinners?"

The priest chuckled. "Everyone is a sinner, but not in the way you've been led to believe. And no soul is hopeless."

"Knowing we are born in sin," he continued, "is not meant to make you feel small and unworthy. All it means is that you have forsaken your identity with God. Instead of knowing your greatness, you feel you're a separate individual who is saddled with endless worries, fears, problems, and cravings.

"Sin," he said, "is nothing but forgetting your true nature as pure consciousness."

"So why is there so much biblical emphasis on being a sinner?" I asked.

"The Bible reminds us that we are sinners, or separated from God as I prefer to think about it, to inspire us to take action. It's meant to spur us toward union with God which, as I told you, happens when you are able to gather your mind, still your thoughts, and recognize your essential divine nature. When that happens, you no longer have to run around looking for love. Once you become love, you love everything and everyone around you in a most natural way."

"How nice," I said. "But can you please remind me again how it is that we came to be separated from God in the first place?"

"God was one, until he divided Himself into time, space, and all of creation. He became all of the objects in the universe, including us. Our sense of individuality is our original sin, to the extent that we have forgotten our true nature as divine consciousness. All of it is nothing but a divine sport where God hides Himself from Himself in order to find Himself again."

"So our fall from grace, our so-called original sin, happened on purpose?"

"It couldn't be any other way, since nothing happens against His will. It's by His own will that He divided Himself into countless forms, granting each soul free will and concealing His state of perfect oneness from Himself. It's by the same act of will, or what we call grace, that a way has been set down for us to recover our unity with God."

"Stilling the mind?" I said.

"You need to understand that stilling the mind is the final step. It's a long journey that begins with faith, prayer, Bible study, contemplation, and living right until the day arrives where intense longing for God causes the mind to let go of everything and become still."

I thought about it for a second, remembering all the talk of sin and punishment that I had listened to in church as a young girl.

"This is quite different from the concept of sin I grew up with, which just made me feel guilty about everything," I said. "When I complained of my guilty feelings, I was told that guilt is good because it acts like the rails on a bridge that stop us from driving off the cliff."

"Guilt may serve that purpose in the short term. But if you believe you're a hopeless sinner, then that belief is only going to make you feel bad about yourself, which will compel you to engage in even worse behavior. There's an old saying which suggests feeling guilt is worse than doing wrong, because if you think you're hopeless or condemned, you have nothing more to lose so you'll act in a hopeless manner. At the same time, ignoring feelings of guilt is not an invitation to behave recklessly. God will make us account for each and every action. It's important to start by loving yourself, and forgiving yourself, knowing you are a child of God no matter what you've done. Only then will you feel empowered to move in the right direction, to live a pure and moral life, knowing the Lord loves you unconditionally."

"If God loves unconditionally, then why would he create the burning fires of hell? That doesn't seem very loving and forgiving."

"As I've explained before, as long as a soul feels it's separate from God, it must reap the fruits of its actions. That is the unshakable divine law. But even the soul that suffers the agonies of hell is not for a moment forsaken by God. The Lord still loves that soul unconditionally, for God is love itself. When those sins are finally spent, God will release that soul from hell."

"Well, to me that means that we're all destined for hell since I don't know a single person who is sinless."

The priest chuckled again. "Not all sins are dealt with through the cleansing fires of hell. People are suffering right here in this world, reaping the fruits of their past actions. But there's an exception to the law of cause and effect. Those who sincerely repent before they die, asking for mercy and forgiveness and absorbing their minds in Christ, will be spared from much of their suffering, if not all of it. Remember, God is most interested in the purity of your heart. He is quick to forgive even at the first signs of repentance, as long as it is heartfelt."

The priest took a moment to catch his breath. "Even if we are forced to suffer the pains of hell, we should do so joyfully, knowing we are the author of our own misfortune. God hasn't wished it upon us, and at the right time, He will redeem us once again."

As I sat in the darkness, I was surprised to find myself contemplating his words as if I truly believed them.

"Coming back to love," I said, "are you saying there's no hope for ordinary love unless we're so spiritually evolved that our love becomes divine?"

"Not quite. Understand that love is not like money that flows back and forth between people, where sometimes you have more and other times less. Love is the deepest part of your being. Instead of looking at people as necessary for you to feel love, look upon them as God's children, knowing that the light behind their eyes is God's light. If you can practice seeing the divine in others, a harmonious current will begin to flow, and you'll begin to experience pure love."

I shook my head, knowing that there wasn't a chance in heaven I would become so pure as to be able to love everyone indiscriminately. I was no Mother Teresa, that much I knew. My mind was judgmental, sarcastic, even cynical. But I liked what the priest said about starting by loving yourself. That was something I could work on.

24

BLACK RIBBON

*S*ending Anthony and Claire on a cruise proved to be the right decision. When they got back, they were both beaming.

"You should have been there," Anthony said as we kissed. "Not a drop of rain."

"I want to go on the cruise to Alaska," Claire said.

"Hey, one thing at a time," Anthony jumped in.

I had heard of the famed cruises to Alaska, which were supposed to be breathtaking.

"If I ever go on a cruise, that would be the one."

"Well then, it's all worked out," said Anthony. "Next year, when all this is behind us, we'll hop on the boat."

"Sounds like a plan." I smiled.

The surgery to remove my thyroid went off without a hitch. After falling under general anesthesia, a three-and-a-half-inch incision was made across my neck just beneath my Adam's apple. The gland was removed, my neck was sutured, and I was wheeled into the recovery room.

I woke up free of pain, thanks to the drugs dripping through my IV, and I enunciated a few words to make sure my vocal cords hadn't been damaged. But when I tried to swallow, my throat barely moved and I knew it would only get worse once those pain meds began to wear off.

In the morning, after I demonstrated to the nurse that I was able to swallow solid food, I was allowed to pack up and go home.

"One more tumor down," said Anthony as we pulled out of the parking lot. I gave a slight nod because my throat ached too much for me to say anything.

The next morning after my shower, I stood in front of my mirror to inspect my incision. The black stitches and swollen scar tissue made me look like Frankenstein's monster, and my eyes moistened with the thought that this cancer was literally cutting me up. I vowed to keep pushing against it as hard as I could.

I dipped my fingers into a jar of white petroleum jelly and applied it over the incision, which felt numb to the touch. Although I knew the scar would eventually fade down to a thin line which no one would notice, I had to laugh at myself for worrying about my appearance when I was in the midst of fighting for my life.

After resting for another week, I headed back to Mass General to undergo another round of scans and to meet with Dr. Yoshimura. He examined my scar and joked that Anthony now had more reasons than ever to buy me beautiful scarves.

We settled down and turned our minds to the protocol that was next on my list. He chose a new drug that worked by activating my T-cells and kicking my immune system into high gear so it could break down my cancer cell barriers and destroy them. Or at least that was the hope.

We reviewed the grim list of potential side effects, which included life-threatening inflammation of various internal organs, as well as discussing treatment basics. The protocol was designed as an outpatient procedure administered intra-venously once every three weeks for a total of four doses. Each session would last around ninety minutes, which was great because it meant Anthony and I no longer had to worry about bunking up at the hospital for a week at a time or making special arrangements for Claire.

Dr. Yoshimura walked me through the treatment in his usual upbeat tone. Although he put me at ease, his habit of sugarcoating everything didn't give me any comfort. I knew if this latest medication failed to kill my remaining tumors, I would be staring down a dark road of dwindling options. In other words, no matter how well I was progressing, this was my last shot at getting into remission.

As I sat in the armchair, I noticed a large poster pinned to the wall behind Dr. Yoshimura's desk which showed a gaunt, but smiling, man in his thirties wearing black boxing gloves. To his side was a large black cancer awareness ribbon and the caption "Let's Knock Melanoma Out! Fundraising Drive 2009, Massachusetts General Hospital." At the bottom it read "Ste-fano Koteas, melanoma survivor." I stared at the man's white teeth and secretly hoped that I, too, could be so lucky.

When my scans showed that my remaining tumors were holding steady, I signed a medical waiver clearing me to begin the first round of infusions. With my treatment details mapped out, I felt ready to visit the office.

∾

I was surprised by how nervous I was when I stepped through the front door of the Dana-Farber Cancer Center. I couldn't believe that a full five months had gone by since I had last been at work.

I chewed my nails while waiting for the elevator to arrive, and the soft fuzz of new hair growing under my kerchief was beginning to itch. I scurried down the hall to my office hoping to arrive unseen, but, as people turned to look, their faces broke out into oh-my-God-you're-back expressions. After a few minutes, about twenty-five people crowded outside my door, and I spent the next half hour greeting and hugging everyone on my wing.

Dr. Connor cut his way through the crowd and emerged into my office.

"Laura! If you had told me you were coming today, I would have organized something," he said, giving me a hug.

I shook my head.

"How are you feeling?"

"Better."

Dr. Connor nodded. He smiled and looked me straight in the eye. "So, are you back?"

"I hope so. It all depends on how I react to my next treatment."

"All right. Drop by my office when you have a moment to fill me in."

And so, without further ado, I found myself back at work almost as if nothing had happened. I sat for a few minutes, observing my desk and reacquainting myself with the rows of heavy binders and color-coded stacks of papers. I sighed, knowing that the next few weeks would involve a terrible amount of catching up. But as daunting as it felt to be back at work, I was thrilled to have come this far. A sudden pride for making it through chemo rushed through me. It was the same feeling I sometimes detected in my young patients—a sense of peace and joy that comes from surviving a grueling ordeal—and I relished the moment for as long as I could.

THE SIXTH VISIT

I kissed Anthony goodbye and stood on our porch as he loaded his suitcase onto his truck. He was flying off to Toronto for a week to meet with Celestica Corporation, which was interested in his latest generation LEDs.

The following Tuesday, I drove myself to the hospital for my first infusion. For the next couple of days, I monitored myself for any adverse reactions, but everything was fine. Yet as the days rolled by, I began to feel more tired than usual, with waves of fatigue like those I experienced during chemo, though much less severe. Back at the office, I realized my concentration was wavering when Dr. Roberts, another member of my team, asked me the same question twice. It made me doubt the wisdom of returning to work while in the midst of my treatment. Exhausted, I decided to head home. Three blocks down, I turned the car around on an impulse and drove to the church to visit the priest.

"May our Lord Jesus Christ bless you and keep you forever," his voice intoned.

"It's good to be here, Father."

But instead of asking me how I was doing, he remained silent, waiting for me to express my latest doubt.

"I've been wondering," I said. "Why is it that our bodies get sick? Why is it that the one thing I need in order to live is trying to destroy itself? Why would nature do that?"

"That's why it's said the body is as good as dead," he replied. "From the moment it is born, the body is nothing except a living corpse, because everything that lives must die. Always remember, my child, that the current of life within is what animates the body, just as the hand animates the glove."

"But that doesn't explain why my body is destroying itself before its time."

The priest sighed. Yet I sensed no judgment, only compassion. "I already told you that your illness was meant to enable you to turn your mind to higher things," he said.

"That's a nice rationalization, even though it's cruel at heart," I said. "It doesn't work when you apply it to children who don't have any intellectual concept about higher things such as God. How do you justify their illnesses?" I pressed.

"Don't underestimate how aware of God children can be, even at a young age. Children intuitively know they came from somewhere greater than this world, although spiritual awareness is not the main reason why some children are destined to die young."

"Then why?"

"We've spoken about this before. The Lord's plans are not meant to be read like an open book. We must have faith in the goodness of His works. The death of a child affects not only the child, but also the people around it, and only God knows what is being accomplished. This is the best answer I can offer. Other answers may make us feel better, but they are empty speculation. In your case, I am convinced your suffering is primarily for the sake of your spiritual growth."

"Even if that is true, why does the lesson have to be so severe? I only have one body."

"Yes, exactly. A body is something you have. It's not you."

"Father, you know what I mean."

"No. Don't miss this opportunity to learn something. Just look around you. The world is full of people dying before their time at every hour. Do you think it's an accident or an act of cruelty by an uncaring God?

"What it teaches," he continued, "is that the body is not that important in God's eyes. Even Lord Jesus only held on to his body for a mere thirty-three years. So it doesn't matter if a person lives three, ten, or one hundred years. Since the soul is immortal, the death of the body is rather inconsequential. It's like tossing aside an old coat only to put on a new one."

"But that's not our everyday experience," I said.

"You're right. Everyone is afraid to die. Fear is quite natural as long as you believe the body to be you. But as I've said before, you are not the body. You are the indwelling consciousness which is aware of the body and the mind, and that awareness, that sense of identity, cannot be buried or burned."

"So I shouldn't care whether I live or die?"

"You can't help but care, because you are not yet spiritually evolved. Even if you pretend not to care, it would be a lie. Only highly evolved souls can overcome the fear of death."

"So where does that leave me?"

"It leaves you with the ability to have faith in the Lord, knowing that nothing can destroy you, and to practice surrendering to His will even as you strive to get better. Remembering death enables you to grow in detachment."

"Father, you know me well enough to know I am empty of faith."

"Then I'm afraid you haven't learned anything from coming here."

His rebuke stung because, in truth, I had come to enjoy my

time with the priest. Despite my stubborn atheism, I no longer
felt conflicted spending time with a man of faith. On the
contrary, I had grown attached to my visits.

"Father, if the body is of so little significance, why would
Jesus take on a body and suffer so much because of it?"

"The body is of little significance from the perspective of the
immortal soul, but it's extremely precious from the point of
view of allowing us to spiritually evolve. This body, which only
produces waste and begins to stink if not bathed once a day, is
at the same time a divine vessel that enables the soul to become
one with God. It's the human body, with its human intellect,
which makes it possible for the soul to move beyond material
existence and merge back into God's light."

"How so?"

"Only a human intellect possesses sufficient self-awareness
to allow it to transcend itself. Wherever the mind goes, the soul
follows. If a mind becomes absorbed in God, the soul merges in
God. Since the body houses the mind, it's our sacred duty to
care and look after our body."

"The body is the temple of God," I said.

"Not only is it the temple of the Holy Spirit, it's the only
place where the Lord shines in His fullness—right in the breast
of every man, woman, and child. The gold and marble temples
built in the name of the Lord, no matter how much they glitter,
are dead and empty compared to the direct presence of God,
which lives in the heart of each human being."

"So the body can be discarded like an old coat, yet, at the
same time, it's the most valuable thing in existence?" I asked.

"Precisely. It's a great paradox, one of God's deepest myster-
ies. The lesson here is to respect and take care of your body as
best you can, while not becoming too attached to something
which is not really you."

"That's easier said than done."

"My child, no one expects you to master something just

because you've heard it once. It takes years, lifetimes, in fact, for these seeds of knowledge to sprout and blossom.

"For the time being," he continued, "be kind to yourself, and try to allow a little peace to enter your mind by accepting that your body can die at any moment even as you fight to keep it alive. You should strive to go beyond your attachment to this fleeting life by remembering you are much greater than this body of ash. Pretending death doesn't exist only makes it more difficult in the end. Believe me, for I have seen it countless times before."

26

THAT'S THE SPIRIT

The next day, as I breathed in the steam rising from my cup of tea, I received a text from Anthony that read *Got it! Contracts signed.*

I smiled at the good news, knowing that the road ahead had gotten just a little smoother. After Anthony got back, he took his new contracts to the bank and demanded they extend his line of credit from three to ten months. They settled for eight, good enough to keep the lights on at his plant until he secured a few more international customers.

"You know, Toronto is a really nice city," he said. "The restaurants are surprisingly good. It kind of reminds me of Chicago. It's a hundred times safer than Chicago but not as nice. Chicago's waterfront is much nicer."

"That's good to know," I said.

"You should see the CN Tower. It's something to behold when you stand at the bottom and look up."

"Uh-huh," I said.

"You're not even listening, are you?"

I lifted my eyes from my case report forms and smiled. Then my face turned pale.

"What's wrong?" he said.

"Nothing. I just have to run to the toilet."

My attack of diarrhea only lasted a few days, but it was rough. When I reported it to Dr. Yoshimura, he didn't sound too concerned.

"That's the new treatment saying hello to you," he joked. "If it comes back, or you bleed from down there, let me know right away," he said, shifting his tone.

Two weeks later, I underwent my second infusion. Around seventy-two hours later my diarrhea came back with a vengeance. I ran to the kitchen cabinet and swallowed two anti-diarrhea pills, but the effects were negligible. When I saw blood in my stools, I knew I had a problem.

"Let's schedule a colonoscopy to make sure the medication hasn't led to ulcerative colitis," said Dr. Yoshimura while I sat in his examination room.

When I informed him that my urine had turned a dark shade of orange, he assured me he would run extra blood and liver function tests.

The colonoscopy itself was pretty easy, except for the part about having to drink an entire gallon of the most awful-tasting solution prior to the procedure. Though some inflammation was visible, he found no bleeding ulcers on the lining of my bowels, which meant I didn't have colitis. Instead, it appeared that my repeated runs to the toilet had caused some capillaries to rupture, which explained the blood I saw. As for my liver test, the results showed that my bilirubin levels were higher than normal. While concerning, those results were not serious enough to halt my treatment.

"Looks like the infusions are testing your limits," Dr. Yoshimura said.

"As bad as it is, compared to the chemo, this is a walk in the park," I replied.

"That's the spirit," he said.

27

HIGH STAKES

The next six weeks were uneventful, which came as a relief to all of us. I underwent my final infusions and watched the skin on my legs dry up and crack before coming off in large white flakes. But it didn't hurt, despite how gruesome it looked.

Since I was feeling better, I slowly eased back into work. As life returned to a semblance of normality, I began to forget about the priest. In truth, I subconsciously avoided going anywhere near Mass General because my upcoming scans would reveal if the protocol had done its job. I knew as a cancer physician that if the treatment had failed to push me into remission, my expected survival rate was minimal at best. Any other treatment of last resort might extend my life for a handful of months, perhaps a year, but, from then on, my statistical chances of remission would be quite slim.

Knowing this, I wasn't surprised when a severe anxiety attack gripped me the night before my scans. It wasn't an irrational, claustrophobic kind of attack that cancer patients sometimes get just from being in the fight for so long. I was gripped instead by the cold, hard realization that I was about to learn whether I was going to live or die, like a murder defendant who is ordered to stand up to receive the jury's verdict.

I spent the following day at the hospital undergoing new scans and having every inch of my body reexamined for suspicious moles. When I informed Dr. Yoshimura of my anxiety issue, he promised that he would try to get the lab results back as soon as possible. Forty-eight hours later, a text message popped up on my phone that I would never forget: *Results in! Good news! Smile! You can come in now.*

I breathed a deep sigh of relief. Anthony dropped what he was doing and raced to the office to pick me up. As we drove, we didn't as much as utter a peep to each other. The stakes were too high and too real for us to comfort each other with hopeful words. All that mattered was getting to the truth.

When I walked into Dr. Yoshimura's office, he didn't waste a second.

"You're NED! You have No Evidence of Disease!" he shouted, opening his arms wide as if he wanted to give me a bear hug.

Normally I would have burst into tears but, oddly, this time I felt nothing. I kept waiting for the emotions to rush forth, but I was only met by a calm and unworldly detachment, as if I were floating in a dream. I wouldn't exactly say that I went numb, but it came close.

I guess my nerves were too raw and I was too overwhelmed to feel anything.

"Did you hear what I said? You're NED!" he repeated, waving his hand in front of my face.

I can't say I remember what happened next.

28

FLOWERS AND CARDS

*a*s it turned out, my tumors had completely vanished. The nodule in my left lung had disappeared as well as the spot in my ascending colon. The treatment had shrunk them to nothing. Only a small bundle of tissue remained in my clavicular lymph node, but another fine needle biopsy confirmed that it was nothing except dead cancer cells. I was termed a "complete responder," one of only a handful of patients who thoroughly respond to the drug.

I was in the clear, at least for the time being.

The three of us celebrated that night by booking a reservation at Mistral, one of my favorite restaurants. I splurged on rock crab ravioli, Dover sole, and the best crème brûlée I've ever had. Outside, sudden gusts lifted the December snow into sparkling whirlwinds, casting a shimmering white frame around the Christmas tree standing by the window. The timing couldn't have been better. My hair had grown back, and when I saw myself reflected in the bathroom mirror dressed in my favorite black dress and Tiffany necklace, I felt alive again. I had to scramble for a tissue to wipe away my tears before they ruined my makeup.

To be declared NED was the greatest gift in the world. Even though we all knew any cancer, especially melanoma, could rear its ugly head at any time, at least now I had been given a second chance. I had achieved a foothold in life, and it gave me the right to believe that I would still be around in three, five, or ten years down the road.

From that point on, unless something changed, I would only have to get scanned every three months. If things held steady for five years, my odds of a relapse were low. All of a sudden, I was able to envision a normal, healthy life. And that feeling, compared to the dread of living with cancer, was simply indescribable.

Anthony and I spent New Year's Eve at home, watching the ball drop over Times Square, while Claire was at a house party with her friends. After we counted down the seconds and kissed, sipping from our champagne flutes, I didn't know whether to laugh or cry. My remission had given me back the promise of life, but getting there had stripped so much away. I was no longer able to plan ahead with any certainty in the way I was accustomed to, because everything could change at a moment's notice.

Life goes on, I told myself.

"Happy New Year!" said Anthony, his face beaming.

"Happy New Year," I replied.

When I showed up to work the following week, I discovered my office was filled with flowers and cards. Gifts and congratulations poured in all day.

The clinical trial of Navatinib, targeting a stem cell regulator gene, had started showing remarkable results. Unlike the previous generation of drugs, which focused on killing cancer cells through a mix of toxic cocktails, this new medicine worked by turning off a single gene that allowed the tumors to divide and grow. So while we had to wrestle with some mild adverse reactions, our little patients were showing such an unprecedented reduction of their cancerous white blood cells that I wondered whether we had stumbled upon the Holy Grail. On top of that, I was riding on such an emotional high from my own remission that I began to believe we were on the cusp of confining acute lymphoblastic leukemia to the dustbin of diseases past, like smallpox or polio. My faith at that point in the power of a good scientific protocol was limitless. To my rose-tinted eyes, anything was possible, although I lamented the fact that nothing like this existed for melanoma.

I got home just after midnight and found Claire asleep on the sofa with the TV on. Since my remission, she was more upbeat than I had seen her in a long time, although with every victory came a new problem. Claire had started seeing a boy named Greg Dyson, who Anthony knew had a bad reputation around school. He'd found out when Greg drove up to the house one Saturday morning in a beat-up Ford Mustang.

"Is that who I think it is?" Anthony had asked, pushing the door open into Claire's room.

"What's the problem?" she said, jumping up from her bed and grabbing her purse.

"Hold on," Anthony said, blocking the door.

"Please, Dad. I don't have time for this!"

"I know who he is, and he's not the kind of guy you want to hang out with."

Claire rolled her eyes. "Sure, Dad. Whatever you say," she'd said, pushing past him.

I turned the TV off and was about to wake her up when I took a moment to observe her peaceful countenance. In sleep, all her problems seemed to have melted away. Although the joy of my recovery had rubbed off on her, Anthony still struggled with her academics, sometimes having to confiscate her cellphone to make sure she finished her homework. Those episodes usually ended in predictable tantrums and door slams which, sadly, had become all too common.

A few days later, Anthony pulled out a folded piece of paper while we all sat around the dinner table.

"What do you have?"

He waved the paper in his hand. "Tickets, tickets."

"Tickets to what?" Claire asked.

"Not to what, to where."

When he said that, my spirits sank.

"Where?" asked Claire.

Anthony looked at me and smiled. "I've decided that over the February break we should go and visit a special place without too much sun, of course, to celebrate Laura's victory against that devil called cancer."

"Where already?" Claire asked, insistent.

"Iceland."

"Iceland!" screamed Claire. "I'll freeze to death!"

"Well, it's not much colder than Boston, but they have these amazing hot springs—"

When Anthony noticed that I hadn't said anything, he looked at me and tipped his head.

"What now?"

"It's a great idea," I said, "but let's talk about it later."

I smiled again because I didn't want to say any more in front of Claire. After she had excused herself, I spoke up.

"Look, I appreciate what you're doing, but—"

"Don't even start," he said, raising his hands in the air.

"I know what you're trying to do," I replied. "I get it, and I love you for it, but it's just not the right time."

"Let me guess. Duty calls."

"Yes. Things are incredibly busy and exciting at the moment. The wind is in my sails and there is so much—"

Anthony slammed his fist on the table. "What kind of a

person are you? You just survived cancer, remember? I'm trying to celebrate with you, as a family, and you're pushing me away.

"If this is how it's going to be," he yelled, "why the hell did you get involved with me in the first place?"

I looked down. He was right, but that didn't mean I was going to take the trip.

"I'm sorry," I said. "I know it looks like I don't care, but I do. If you could only step into my shoes. The trial ends in early March, so if I go on this trip now, A, I won't enjoy it because I'll be thinking about work, and, B, I'll just fall behind again."

"We're talking just over a week here for crying out loud."

"I know, but a lot can happen in ten days. That's just the way it works when you're in the eye of the hurricane. I just can't take off so close to the end of the trial."

"As soon as it's over," I said, "I promise we'll catch the first flight out of here."

"We can't leave in March when Claire is in the middle of classes," he said.

"When is her next break?"

"Mid-April."

"So we'll go then."

"Sure," he said, drawing the word out. "Then you'll come up with another bullshit excuse, like you need to write your damn paper or God knows what."

"Can we drop the cursing?" I asked.

"You know, just a few months ago, you were lying on a bed looking like the end was near."

I nodded my head. "I know. And after the study closes out, we're out of here. I promise."

Anthony shot me a look of disgust and ripped up the reservations before throwing the scraps of paper at me.

29

MOTHER

*M*y refusal to take time off not only put a chill between me and Anthony, it didn't ingratiate me with Claire either. I knew my stubbornness came off as callous and insensitive, but Anthony didn't realize I truly was in the midst of a game changer. Everyone at Dana-Farber was hyper-motivated by the kind of results we were seeing, starting with Dr. Connor, and there was no way I was going to miss a day of what was, without question, the most important work of my career. Besides, Anthony and Claire had recently returned from a Caribbean cruise, so it wasn't like I was depriving them of some long-awaited break.

For the following three nights, Anthony took Claire out on the town because he was too upset to be around me. With the house to myself, I indulged in the small luxury of soaking in an Epsom salt bath, wishing that Anthony would appreciate that in my line of work real lives were at stake. The lives of children, no less. The clinical trial was not a dry run, and saving lives was more pressing to me than the joys of exploring Iceland. As I stood before the mirror, wrapping a towel around my hair, I searched for a better way to make Anthony understand how much I cared about him. About us.

When the doorbell rang, I took a deep breath before turning the handle.

"Mother."

I had decided it was high time for my mother to visit. I hadn't seen her in almost two years, and I was surprised by how frail she appeared. She looked so thin under her blue cardigan.

I stepped onto the porch to hug her while Anthony brought in her suitcases.

"You look different," she said.

"I know," I replied.

We sat around the fireplace, catching up over tea and butter cookies. As soon as I gathered the courage, I mentioned that I had something important to share with her.

"Are you planning to get married?" she asked.

"No, Mother, it's nothing like that. You see, ten months ago, I was diagnosed with cancer." Her face turned to stone when I said the word "cancer."

"What do you mean cancer? What do you mean ten months ago? Why on God's earth didn't you tell me?"

I spent the next two hours apologizing and going over every detail of my ordeal, reassuring her again and again that all was well. As I spoke, my mother's left hand would twitch, probably from anger. At other times, she just lowered her head to dab her eyes with her handkerchief. I explained that I had kept the diagnosis a secret, not only for her sake but because I didn't think I could have coped if she had seen me so sick.

"Well, it's totally unacceptable," she cried.

"I'm sorry," I repeated. "But please understand, I didn't want to worry about you while you worried over me."

"You know, Laura, it's not always about you. This is cancer we're talking about, not a common cold. As your mother, I have every bloody right to worry over you whether you like it or not."

"I'm sorry."

"From now on, I expect to hear from you every week. If anything should change, even the slightest thing, God help you if I don't hear from you," she stammered.

"It was a mistake," I whispered back.

30

THE SEVENTH VISIT

*I*t took a few days for my mother to adjust to my new reality, along with a call from Dr. Yoshimura to convince her that I was truly classified as NED.

We spoke for hours on end: stories about Dad, memories from my childhood, our hopes for the future. We laughed and cried, and by the end of the week, my diagnosis had brought us closer than we had been in a long time. Perhaps waiting to stave off this cancer before telling her had been the right decision after all. Now we could both relax and look ahead, skipping all the torment and sleepless nights. As I had learned by working with the heartbroken parents of my child patients, sometimes it's necessary to manage how and when the truth is revealed.

I forced back my tears when we dropped my mother off at the airport. To make it up to her, I promised we would fly up to Portland at some point in the summer.

Two weeks later, while I was in the middle of my patient rounds, a code blue alert sounded throughout the hospital for a patient in the adult ward two floors up. No matter how many times I heard the drone-like recording, it always stopped me in my tracks. My instinct was to drop everything and run to help, even though we were expected to carry on with whatever we were doing and let a specialized team deal with such emergencies.

A black cassock blurred past me a minute into the code blue. It was Father Lacey, the hospital chaplain, running to the stairs. One never knew during a code blue whether a patient would be successfully resuscitated or not, which left precious minutes for Father Lacey to utter the last rites when all hope was gone. When I caught a glimpse of him, my thoughts turned to my priest, if I could call him that. It occurred to me that after all of the patience he had shown me, dropping out of sight had been rather inconsiderate.

As soon as the commotion settled, I promised myself that before the end of the week I would set aside a couple of hours to drive to the church.

On Friday afternoon, I found an opportunity. After a long meeting with Dr. Connor and our co-investigators, I managed to escape while the others scrambled for a late lunch.

"May our Lord Jesus Christ bless you and keep you," the priest whispered.

"Father, it's been a long time since I visited."

"I'm only a servant, waiting on you," he said.

"I have wonderful news," I began. "I'm officially in remission."

"Then God has answered all our prayers."

"I guess he has," I whispered, thinking in reality that the drugs had cured me, not God.

The priest remained silent. Only the sound of his breathing filled the air.

"Now that I'm better," I said, breaking the silence, "I wanted to thank you for giving me so much of your time."

"My child, it's fine to rejoice at the news of your health. But don't let your happiness blind you to the lessons God is trying to teach you," he said.

That sure sounded like a bit of a downer, I thought to myself. After barely surviving chemotherapy, I was expecting the priest to be a little more upbeat.

"If there are lessons to be learned, why are they always so hidden?"

The priest laughed. "They are only hidden if we don't have the eyes to see them."

"Enlighten me then."

"You tell me. What has your brush with death taught you?"

I was taken aback by his choice of words, which I found rather insensitive.

"I learned that it's awful to lie helpless and in so much pain. That it's easy to tell others to be strong, but not so easy to do yourself. I learned that I want to live because I have so much left to accomplish and that—"

"Ambitions and desires," he interrupted. "They're never-ending, aren't they? Even when life itself flashes before our eyes.

"Most people," he continued, "realize how precious time is when faced with their own mortality."

I felt mildly annoyed. "Father, with all due respect, after everything I've lived through, I'm well aware of how precious time is."

"If you had really understood, you would have lost interest in your old ambitions. After a brush with death, wise souls shift their focus to more important things like love, peace, and drawing near God's light."

"That sounds very nice, but when I get up in the morning, I have to do something with my time. I can't just sit around all day thinking about love, peace, and God's light, can I?" I said. "It doesn't exactly pay the rent."

The priest breathed out a long sigh. "I'm not suggesting that you shouldn't apply yourself to your work. 'By the sweat of your brow you will eat your food,' says the Book of Genesis. Drawing near God's light is meant to nurture faith and help one practice surrender—things we've already discussed. By all means, continue to work, but while going about your tasks, keep the Good Lord at the center of your mind and offer all of your work in His name."

"I don't even understand what that means," I said.

"It means you do your best while surrendering the fruits of your work to Him. You dedicate all your efforts to Him, knowing it's only through His grace that you are able to work in the first place. Whether you succeed or not is of far less importance."

"I see."

"Instead of chasing after your usual desires," he said, "use the time you have left to focus on what God wants most, which is for you to make the conscious effort to fill your heart with His blissful presence. If you persist in remembering Him, you'll come to experience an abiding happiness that lacks the emptiness which always follows even the greatest of achievements."

I had to admit to myself that every time I achieved something, even things I had worked on for years, the satisfaction was always short-lived. My mind would start thinking about my next conquest.

"That emptiness. What causes it?"

"It's the nature of the mind to be restless. Left to its own devices, the mind would be unsatisfied even if it devoured the entire universe. Only when we force it to turn its attention inward does it calm down and discover the peace it was always searching for."

"But the desire to accomplish new things is one of the qualities that makes us great," I protested.

"That might be true from an ordinary perspective," he said,

"but not from a spiritual point of view. The endless chase after the next great thing occupies the mind, while denying it the chance to slow down and experience the divine peace it craves. In the name of progress, people have grown distracted, arrogant, and self-absorbed, and they're beginning to lose their ability to empathize with others. They are unable to focus on anything for more than a few seconds at a time. We would feel more fulfilled if we limited our desires to a few that matter, while making some time for quiet contemplation, recognizing that God wants more from us than a show of external success."

"But if I spend all day thinking about God, nothing will get done."

"Don't misunderstand. Surrender to God doesn't make you dull or lethargic. On the contrary, if you align yourself with God's will, you'll discover there's no end to what you can achieve. You become much more powerful. As you go about your life's work, just remember to include God in it. That's the true meaning of approaching the Lord on a bended knee. Humility gives rise to gratitude, which in turn attracts God's grace."

"I'll try to throw out some gratitude to the universe," I quipped.

The priest ignored me. "The mind is like a crystal that takes on the color of whatever comes near it. If you dwell on greed, you will become seized by greed. If you dwell on anger, you will become seized by anger. If you dwell on grief, you will become the victim of grief. But if you dwell on God, you will become the embodiment of purity, love, and peace," he said, his voice filled with compassion. "So before you allow yourself to get carried away by hopes and ambitions, however noble they may be, try to remember the deeper purpose of your life."

"Remind me," I said.

"To recognize your absolute oneness with God," he

answered. "You know," he said, "there's a good reason why our lives are so short. If we were able to live forever, time would have no value. We would find ourselves adrift in an endless stream of material existence. Allotting us a fixed number years forces us to ask the important questions: Who am I? What am I doing here? What is the ultimate purpose of my life? It's another of God's mercies that even though our souls are eternal, our births into these bodies of flesh and blood are marked by certain death. Our fear of death is what makes us turn to our highest duty, which is to absorb our hearts and minds in Christ.

"Without death, time would stretch on forever, and we would always chase after this or that, while sleepwalking through life. We would remain trapped in an endless physical dream that we wouldn't be able to or wouldn't want to wake up from, unable to sense the distance between us and the peace that is God's light. That's why time is so precious, and why death can be viewed as a blessing. Death limits time, and that limit ultimately forces us to awaken to God's presence."

I sat there, trying to absorb all the teachings he was lobbing at me.

"But what about those who die suddenly without warning?" I asked.

"It's not the moment of death that matters. The lesson lies in knowing we are all going to die one day or another and that our time is precious. Everyone knows they are going to die, but few choose to turn their minds to higher things. Don't be like those people who are asleep while awake. Try to make the most of your time."

When I stepped out of the church into the freezing cold, I felt uneasy and disappointed. I thought the priest would give me a pep talk about how miracles can happen when you never lose hope, or how good my fortune was, or how I had been blessed with a second chance at life. Instead, he had spoken to me about death. Didn't he see that I had gone there to share in my joy?

I shrugged it off and hurried back to my car, cranking up the heat as I drove away. As soon as I had stopped shivering, I began to wonder if my visits to the church were still worth the bother.

THE NEW PROTOCOL

*B*y mid-February, we had regained what felt like the old family rhythm. Anthony had flown down to Mexico on another business trip, which also turned out well. Slowly, but surely, he was turning things around.

"How was it?" I asked as I hugged him at the airport.

"Let's pick Claire up and I'll tell you over dinner," he said, beaming. "How are you feeling?" he added.

The fact that I had not been scanned since December made me nervous. I monitored myself daily without fail, looking for symptoms or unexpected changes, but everything seemed fine. I wasn't sweating at night, I hadn't detected any new lumps, and I wasn't suffering from any unusual pains. I just had to wait for my next scan to confirm that I was in good health.

That Saturday, we decided to drive up to Gloucester for the day, but I couldn't find my lipstick on our way out. I poked around Claire's bedroom, thinking that perhaps she had borrowed it, but found nothing. As I was about to leave, I noticed her backpack slumped in the corner. I hesitated, not wanting to invade her privacy, but rationalized the trespass as harmless if it allowed me to recover my lipstick.

When I unzipped a side pocket, I discovered a half-empty box of laxatives instead of lipstick. I showed the pills to Anthony, who shrugged.

"I guess she's constipated," he said.

"I doubt it. No one takes that many laxatives."

"Then she'll explain it to me when I ask her," he said.

As busy as work had become, little did I know that it was about to get a lot busier. Five minutes into my rounds, I received a text from Dr. Connor informing us that the FDA had decided to conduct a spot audit and to meet him at his office. The purpose of the "bioresearch monitoring program," as it was called, was to verify the integrity of our clinical data and ensure we were complying with all of the regulations. An FDA audit was not in and of itself a bad sign; it just meant we needed to spend an ungodly amount of time organizing the thousands of documents identified for review. We only had five days to get the job done.

When I called Anthony to let him know what was coming, he sounded worried. "Is it safe for you to work so hard?"

"I don't see that I have a choice," I said.

The audit prep turned out to be twice as hard as I thought, and I managed by getting up often from my chair to stretch my legs, drinking lots of fluids, and eating well. The good news was that most of the data binders were in excellent shape. Still, the long hours took their toll, and at one point I became so dizzy and exhausted I had to lie down on a gurney to catch my breath.

After the auditor signed off, I managed by some miracle to drive myself home without getting into an accident. I climbed the stairs, shut the bedroom door and passed out for fourteen hours straight.

The next two weeks went by in relative tranquility until Dr. Connor surprised us with yet another major announcement.

"I know what I'm about to say is unorthodox, but the board and I had a long meeting with Medalux Sciences. In light of the remarkable results we're seeing, we've decided to expand the sample size while keeping to the same end point."

When I heard his words, I was both elated and distraught. Increasing the number of patients mid-trial was seldom done. It required regulatory approval and meant our results to date were promising enough that more patients were needed to ensure our reported outcomes were accurate. The new protocol was proving so effective, Dr. Connor didn't want to take any chances that an inappropriate sample size or some other bias could in any way diminish the value of the data.

All of this translated into additional work signing up new patients and working with the IRB and other authorities to expand the trial on short notice. On the upside, it meant we would receive a lot of attention from our peers as word spread. On the downside, it meant any plans for a vacation in April were off the table. I didn't even want to think of how Anthony and Claire would react.

HOMECREST

*T*he added pressures forced me, once again, to push aside everything that wasn't related to work. As luck would have it, the timing couldn't have been worse. Little did I know that Claire had been busy shooting black-and-white portraits of people around the city for the past month. Her efforts were not for a school project, but to build a college application portfolio. She had even organized an evening at home with her friends to sort through her work, inviting her arts teacher to help her decide which photographs to include. She went on and on about it while Anthony fried his favorite veal and onion steaks.

"Claire," I said, turning to face her, "I think it's great you're taking pictures, but final exams are closer than you realize. If I were you, I'd put all of my energies into my studies. Especially after that last math test. Don't you think your grades are more important?"

Claire stared at me as if she were seeing the devil.

"Why do you have to step on everything I do?" she asked before storming out of the kitchen.

Anthony rubbed his chin. "Can you go easy on her? Just for once. Do you think you can do that?"

"Do you want her to flunk her last year of high school? Because that's what's going to happen if you don't take control," I argued.

As expected, Anthony took her side and set up a white screen and projector in the basement along with a table of catered food.

On Friday afternoon, as I put on my coat to leave the office to attend Claire's event, I received a text from Dr. Roberts asking me to meet him in his office. When I got there, he was hunched over the randomization schedules for the new patients.

"Something's not right," he said. "I was hoping that you could help me review the selection covariates."

"Michael, of all days... There's somewhere I have to be. Can't this wait till tomorrow?"

He looked at me with a blank stare. "Not really. The first infusions start in the morning, and I can't continue unless I'm absolutely sure the randomization is right. You're the only person I trust with statistics," he threw in.

I sighed, wondering if my ease with mathematics was at times more of a curse than a blessing.

"I'd help, but I really have to be somewhere," I repeated.

"Please," he insisted. "It won't take long."

As I feared, "it won't take long" took a long time indeed, long enough for me to miss Claire's event. Analyzing all the variables to ensure each patient was slotted into a proper control group was delicate work, but it was essential to protect the trial's integrity.

In the end, I found nothing wrong with the schedules Dr. Roberts had prepared, despite the fact that a few clusters appeared odd at first glance. As I rushed to the parking lot, I could already hear Anthony's voice ringing in my ears.

I rehearsed my apology even before I stepped through the front door. But when Anthony emerged from the basement carrying a handful of dirty dishes, he simply ignored me.

"I'm sorry—"

"Don't say a word," he said.

I braced myself for a long speech, but, instead of snapping, Anthony smiled and addressed me in a soft tone. "The truth is, we enjoyed it more without you."

Claire surfaced next, just behind her father.

"Claire," I began. But before I could utter another word, she turned around and darted back down into the basement.

I was well aware how my compulsion with work had worn everyone thin. Yet I never blamed Anthony or Claire for resenting me, not for a moment. As I lay in bed, I tried hard to imagine a way to balance my life, but deep down I knew that my professional responsibilities would never ease up. I was simply married to my job.

All of these concerns came to a screeching halt a few weeks later when Anthony called me out of the blue.

"It's Claire," he said in a panic. "We're in the ER. She's having severe abdominal pains."

I hung up the phone and ran to my car. She was lying on a gurney, still bent over with pain when I located them behind a privacy curtain in the emergency room.

"How's she doing?" I asked.

"They're running tests. But if they don't zero in on the problem soon, they're going to send her to the operating room for exploratory surgery," Anthony said.

Claire was lucky it never went that far. In less than an hour, she was diagnosed with nothing more than a mild kidney infection. Yet when the doctors questioned her, it became apparent that Claire had slipped back into the throes of bulimia.

As soon as Claire fell asleep, Anthony and I snuck out of her room for a cup of tea.

"I'm so sorry," I said. "I know I haven't been much of a parent lately, but—"

"It's not always about you," he snapped, taking a page from my mother's book.

After her discharge, Claire never explained what had caused her to relapse, but she hinted it had something to do with a joke Greg made about the size of her thighs. Even so, Anthony and I both knew her problems with self-esteem and her struggles since the death of her mother were the true culprits behind her illness. While in the past she had locked herself in the bathroom to purge, this time she covered her tracks by taking laxatives at school, which made it harder for us to notice she was ill.

Thinking back, when Anthony questioned her about the pills in her backpack, she insisted she had bought them to deal with a bloated stomach, and lied about only taking one.

"I forgot to close my locker and when I got back from class, most of them were gone," was the story she had given.

∼

A few weeks after her scare, Anthony and Claire flew up to the Homecrest Eating Disorders Center in Stowe, Vermont, where she would participate in a fourteen-week program.

That night, he called from his hotel room.

"How's she settling in?" I asked.

"Well enough," he said. "She's not resisting treatment, which is good."

"Good," I echoed.

After an uncomfortable silence, he spoke.

"Look, I'm not blaming you for her problems, but you could have handled her differently."

"I know."

"She always feels judged or rejected when she's around you," he added. "Do you know what she told me the other day?"

"What?"

"That she can't stand seeing your face."

"I guess I earned that," I said. "When are you coming home?" I asked, suddenly feeling low.

"I'm not sure. I need to stick around for a few days, maybe a week, and make sure she settles in okay."

"Of course."

I held my breath for a second, waiting for him to say more. When he didn't, I blurted out, "I don't know if you forgot, but I'm getting scanned on Friday."

"Oh, that's right," he said. "I guess it just slipped my mind."

33

A PART OF THE FAMILY

For the first time since I was diagnosed with cancer, I drove to Mass General to get scanned without Anthony by my side. Three months had passed since I had been declared NED, and it was time to have another look. As always, I felt sick to my stomach even though I told myself there wasn't any reason to be concerned. To my great relief, the CAT scan proved clear. Everything looked exactly as it should.

When Anthony returned from Stowe, he was distant and withdrawn. We spoke at length about Claire, who was making steady progress, and I mentioned a list of changes I planned to make to become a better parent. But he wasn't interested, instead grabbing the remote and raising the volume on the Roy Orbison concert playing on the screen.

In the morning, over bacon and eggs, I tried to get him to open up, but he kept his eye contact to a minimum.

"Please, Anthony. What's on your mind?"

He just shrugged.

"When Claire gets back," I said, "I'm turning over a new leaf. I'll make sure—"

"I guess," he interrupted, "I guess now is as good a time as ever to talk about it."

"I know something is bothering you," I said.

Anthony frowned. He pressed his lips together, flexing his fist two or three times before speaking.

"Laura, I don't know how to say this, but Claire's doctor thinks you're a much bigger part of her bulimia than you realize."

I could sense where this was headed, but instead of defending myself, I remained silent.

"We're not saying you caused her to get sick, but all that pressure you put on her to become a better student backfired. They think it's unhealthy for you to be around her, at least for the time being. I hate to admit it, but you create a lot of stress for her. Stress that's not good."

I nodded quietly, reaching for a napkin to wipe my eyes. Anthony leaned across the table and held my hands.

"I know you've been to hell and back, but she's my daughter. You understand? And you're never going to change."

"Have I been that awful?" I asked. "Is this about the canceled vacation?"

"That's part of it. She knows your intentions are good, but she complains that you're way too intense. She feels like you're attacking her even when you don't say a word."

"What if I just stay out of her way?"

"You're not capable of doing that. It would last a week. And like I said, it's not just what you've said to her. It's also the energy you bring to the house."

"How so?" I asked.

"I'm going to be blunt. I don't feel you've made any real effort to be a part of our family."

Deep in my heart, I couldn't deny what Anthony was saying. I guess never actually raising a child past infancy had blindsided me. I had spent too much time with other A-type personalities, too much time running after my agenda, too much time basking in the glow of my professional achievements, which had left me myopic and sharp-tongued. I expected everyone to think and behave like me, no matter who they were.

"There's another thing," he said. "Your fight against cancer. It's a terrible thing for me to say, but it's made things really heavy for her."

"Anthony, is this what you want?"

He thought about it for a second, pressing his lips even tighter. "I know things can't go on the way they are now. She just can't handle it," he said, shaking his head. "I'm also not happy," he admitted. "I haven't been happy for a long time."

"So what's next?" I asked, wiping fresh tears from my eyes.

"I have no idea," he lied, taking the napkin from my hand and lifting it to his own eyes.

34

BITTERSWEET

$\mathcal{J}$ was restless and disoriented for a couple of days until the idea of moving out started to sink in. Anthony tried to console me by suggesting this was not the end of our relationship, just a time to recalibrate until he could understand how to help Claire. But I knew full well that as soon as I moved out, the feeling that we were a family would begin to fade away.

After much back and forth trying to come up with a compromise, I caved in and agreed to rent a condominium. A few days later I signed a lease for a two-bedroom apartment not far from where I used to live. If the thought of moving wasn't hard enough, Anthony made things worse by insisting that I pack up and leave before Claire returned from her treatment so he could give her a fresh start. He gave me a month.

Moving day was particularly painful. Anthony loaded my belongings into a U-Haul truck and drove me to the new address. As we pulled up to the apartment, I faulted myself for the hundredth time for imposing my views on Claire. Instead of acting as a positive force on her, I achieved the exact opposite. I had let Anthony down when he had taken a chance on me.

He looked over and caught me staring at my hands.

"Laura, if you need anything at all, just pick up the phone," he said, trying to sound upbeat. But his kindness didn't give me any comfort, in fact it made me feel worse. I would have preferred if he had told me up front that it was over between us, but I guess he lacked the courage to face up to it.

~

The month of April was bittersweet. Spring was in the air, and the blooming flowers marked my one-year cancer anniversary. The fact that I was officially in remission twelve months into my diagnosis was certainly cause for celebration. But it was all overshadowed by my breakup with Anthony, who, despite everything, insisted on taking me out for dinner to celebrate.

The months came and went. By late June, Claire was back in the house, her illness again under control. Anthony had also managed to score a major victory when he convinced her school to allow her to take her finals in July, making it possible for her to graduate. As I had anticipated, I saw little of Anthony. Yet as much as I missed living with him, I had to admit, despite moments of sadness, that I enjoyed the freedom of coming and going whenever I pleased. My newfound freedom was a rediscovered pleasure, not unlike stumbling across a favorite old song.

~

In August of 2010, our clinical trial entered its final weeks, and our outcomes were unprecedented. Many of our little patients had achieved remission at record speeds, with less than a handful unresponsive to the protocol, which meant that everything Dr. Connor and I had dreamed of was coming true. On one occasion, after examining a blood sample, Dr. Connor smiled and commented that I had arrived on the scene at exactly the right time because this was without question the defining moment of his career. A few days later, he sat me down in his office and slid a letter across the desk which formally offered me a permanent staff position at the Center.

That night, despite my elation, I decided to forgo the invitations to celebrate and chose instead to curl up on my sofa with my favorite glass of wine. A quiet mood had descended over me, and I wasn't the least interested in being the object of anyone's attention. As I thought about it, I realized the offer marked the end of a long and difficult chapter in my life, and I needed some alone time to take it all in.

As I sat in my bare-walled living room, flipping through the channels, I admitted to myself that the joys of being single were quickly wearing off, and I was starting to miss Anthony. The grass is always greener on the other side of the fence, I thought to myself.

I sipped the last of my wine, struggling to keep my eyes open until the sound of the priest's voice exploded into my head and jolted me awake. I stood up, half drunk, and stumbled through the room, realizing that I hadn't thought of the priest in a long time and that his words were beginning to fade away. By the time I reached my bed, it dawned on me that I had never bothered to learn his name or meet him face-to-face. He had been nothing but a disembodied voice, floating through the lattice. As I slipped into unconsciousness, I kept trying to imagine what he might look like.

35

THE EIGHTH VISIT

*W*ith the trial officially over, I poured myself into the peer-reviewed paper that Dana-Farber would submit to *The Lancet*. I was only a few weeks into my first draft when I noticed I was tiring a lot faster than usual. The following afternoon, while standing in line for coffee, my arms broke out with goose bumps. I started to shiver, despite the fact it was comfortably warm inside the hospital cafeteria. Not willing to accept that anything ominous was happening, I just ignored it. Two days later, when I stepped out of the shower, I sensed a slight pain in the back of my left knee. When I reached down to touch it, I discovered to my horror that one of my lymph nodes was tender and swollen.

I called Dr. Yoshimura right away on his private number. Even though it was Sunday, he agreed to meet me that afternoon in his office. As soon as he examined my leg, he picked up the phone to set up urgent CAT and MRI scans.

When the test results came back late that evening, my heart sank.

"Laura, this is hard for me to say, but you have a two-centimeter tumor in one of your popliteal nodes. The good news is that nothing has migrated into your spinal cord or brain."

For the first time since I had met him, Dr. Yoshimura looked somber. All traces of his familiar smile were wiped clean off his face.

"So what now?" I sighed.

"Since we've only detected one new tumor, we have a shot at surgery. We need to remove the nodes in your knee as well as your clavicular nodes as a precaution."

Beyond the surgeries, Dr. Yoshimura decided that the appearance of a new growth so early into my remission meant that he could no longer employ a "wait and see" strategy. The odds were just too high that new tumors would emerge. Instead, he wanted to jump into a dangerous but promising treatment known as adoptive cell transfer with TIL (tumor infil-trating lymphocytes), which was proving effective for some patients. But the TIL protocol was fraught with challenges, starting with the six weeks required to harvest and grow the lymphocyte cells that would be infused into my body. To my mind, six weeks could land me past the point of no return.

A second concern was whether I would have the strength to withstand the high-dose chemotherapy required before the infusions. The chemo was needed to kill off most of the native lymphocyte cells in my bone marrow. Unfortunately, red blood cells are also produced in the bone marrow, and the death of those cells triggers severe side effects, sometimes resulting in death. The need to travel to the National Institutes of Health Clinical Center in Maryland to undergo the procedure, one of only three hospitals in the world that offered it, complicated matters even further.

I sat in Dr. Yoshimura's office, analyzing my options. My ability to survive the chemotherapy was at the top of my mind.

Dr. Yoshimura nodded in agreement. "Yes, the chemo is my biggest worry, but if we move quickly and extract your lymph nodes before the tumor weakens you, I'm confident you'll be strong enough to handle it."

"I'm counting on it," I said. "When can we start?" I added.

"I'll have to contact the folks at NIH to see how busy they are in the lab. As you can imagine, they tend to have a waiting list."

"No doubt," I said. "It's just not what I needed to hear."

Dr. Yoshimura smiled meagerly before glancing away. That simple but telling gesture, coupled with the silence that followed, confirmed to me that I was once again walking on thin ice.

When I stepped into my apartment, I was confused and disoriented. My whole world, which I had struggled so hard to right, had turned upside down again in the blink of an eye. I couldn't believe that my cancer had returned, and a rage rose up in me the likes of which I had never felt before.

I stood by the window, watching a slow-moving line of red taillights wind its way up the street. Inside I was sinking, which gave me the urge to run to the toilet and vomit. After the heaving stopped, I pulled myself up to the sink and brought my mouth to the faucet, letting the cold water soothe my burning throat.

I sat on the sofa, wondering whom to call first, but I just put the phone down and cried. I figured that if I could just make it through the TIL, I had a good chance of living. Although I was hanging by a delicate thread, there was still hope in my heart. And hope was hope, however dim it burned.

I spoke to my mother the next morning, this time without mincing any words. She told me she was getting on the next plane to Boston. Anthony was next. As soon as I told him, he rushed over to console me.

"Let me know what you need," he said.

"Mother is coming, so I'll have more help this time around."

"Good, but don't hesitate to call me."

I walked around the living room in circles after Anthony left, stopping before the cream wooden cabinet. I opened the glass doors and stared at the rows of martini glasses resting on the shelf. They were a picture of elegance, their long stems shining beneath the halogen spotlight. I raised my arm and swept most of them off the shelf, shattering them on the floor. I didn't know what had driven me to violence, other than a deep-seated need to break something. I sat on the sofa and stood up again. I sat back down and chewed on my fingernails. After a few minutes, I gathered the courage to dial Dr. Connor's number. Of all the calls I had to make, this was the one I dreaded most because so much was on the line.

I cut straight to the point. "Brendan, I have terrible news. It looks like a new tumor has surfaced."

Between his expressions of sorrow, I filled him in on the details. I forced myself to sound as positive as I could, reassuring him that the combination of surgery and TIL would allow me to bounce back yet again.

"Of course," he said. "I'm completely behind you. Whatever it takes."

After a long silence, I let him know what was really on my mind.

"The journal paper. You know I'd hate to jeopardize it because of this. I just want to make sure there's still enough time to—"

"Don't even mention it," he interrupted. "Yes, there's a deadline, but we have some wiggle room. We'll hold back for as long as we can. Just focus on getting better and forget about everything else," he insisted.

"Thank you," I whispered, feeling a tinge of relief.

After I hung up, I closed my eyes and cried some more

while Dr. Connor's assurances washed away beneath another wave of despair.

When I woke up, I was still lying on the sofa. The light filtering through the drapes cast a soft orange glow over the furniture. I had slept through the entire day, a coping mechanism I picked up in the days after Elaine's passing when reality was so unbearable that my body would just shut down.

I sat up and rubbed my eyes. Twilight had painted the apartment blue, and all of a sudden, I felt alone and afraid. The real possibility that I might die in the not too distant future flashed through my mind, and I thought back to how the priest had steered our last conversation toward death. Did he know something I didn't? I decided to go back and find out.

When I stepped into the church, I saw that the green bulb above the confessional was already lit.

"May our Lord Jesus Christ bless you and bring you into the Kingdom of Heaven."

"Father, I'm so pleased it's you," I said.

"I am always here, my child."

I sat, quiet for a second, enjoying the sound of his voice.

"Father, I want to tell you that—"

"Let me guess," he jumped in. "Your illness has returned."

"How do you know?" I asked, remembering how blunt he could be.

"Well, I haven't seen you since you told me of your recovery. And now that you're here, it can only mean one thing."

"You're so right," I confessed. "Another tumor has surfaced, but it's going to be removed."

I sensed no reaction from the priest. "How can I help you, my child?" was all he asked.

I hesitated for a moment, searching for the right words.

"Father, I've always secretly believed that I'd beat this. But the truth is, I'm really afraid. I'm afraid of the thought that I might die and all my—"

"Fear of death persists only as long as you believe yourself to be this mere body of flesh and blood," he said. "If you could understand that the soul is more real and lasting than your body, you'd have no reason to fear."

"It's a nice thought, but while I know for a fact that my body exists, I can't or don't know if I have a soul."

"Then have a little faith," he said. "You're so adept at having faith in material science, why not try a little faith in the Lord's Word?"

I nodded. "I wish I could," I whispered.

"If you grasp at something, the fear of losing it is quite natural. Right now you're grasping at your physical body, even though you've known since you were a child that one day you would have to let it go."

I nodded again.

"Think of it this way, the body you identified with as a child no longer exists. Not even your bones are the same. And your current body will one day also cease to exist, yet you insist on calling it you. Isn't that a form of madness? In truth, your existence as a conscious soul will continue without interruption, just as there was no interruption when you transformed from child to adult."

"I agree that the body changes, but as we grow our physical form is always there. In death, the body disappears altogether."

"Yes, it does, but your soul does not. The soul resembles the physical body, and just behind the soul is the eternal awareness we call God. You are all light, nothing but light. From the highest perspective, even your physical body is nothing but light."

"I wish I could accept everything you're saying. Nothing would make me happier."

"Then accept it. There's no need to make things complicated. Remember, everything in God's creation is cyclical. The leaves fall only to grow back again. Day turns into night, which turns back into day. The seasons rotate endlessly. So why do you think it's any different for human beings, who are born into a body which lives, grows, and dies until that soul is reborn into a new body to continue the cycle?"

"That's what you said before."

"And it bears repeating. Death is nothing other than a natural transition. The deeper part of you never dies. No matter how many times you are born and die, you'll forever remain a burning flame of awareness that experiences itself as bliss and peace."

"I wish I could feel some of that peace."

"Then give up your fear, which is like a wall you've built around you that keeps you separate from God. Stop grasping at things that are destined to perish. If you cannot surrender your fear, then at least pray to the Lord. Pray for a peaceful death and to be delivered into His arms. The truth is, you can only be afraid as long as you think you are alone. Loneliness, separateness, and individuality; these are just other words for spiritual ignorance. When you understand that everything moves and exists within God's light, you feel warmth, you feel comfort, you feel safe. Knowing this, you come to understand there is no real perishing when you die. Death is an awakening to a new existence. Hopefully, a better one if you have lived a just and moral life."

"I remember you once told me that people cannot get over their fear of death however hard they try."

"Yes, it's true. Only saints and elevated souls can die without fear because they are the only ones who have realized their unity with God. But for the rest of us, at least knowing we possess an indestructible soul helps. Knowing God will be there to receive us helps. Knowing our minds will continue to function after our bodies die helps. Having faith in His goodness and perfection helps."

"But all of that won't get rid of my fear."

"Then offer your fear at God's feet. Pray for Him to consume your fear. By remembering and holding fast to Jesus' name, we are delivered from all fear."

I nodded again, though I knew the task was beyond me.

"Tell me about Jesus," I asked.

"Jesus was fully aware of his oneness with God, which is why He extols us again and again to give up our individuality, our false belief that we are this body, and rediscover our oneness with the Lord. That's what He meant when He said in Matthew, 'He who has found his life will lose it, and he who has lost his life for My sake will find it.' In other words, he who chases after the life of the body dies, but he who sacrifices his bodily identification and rises as pure awareness regains his eternal life in spirit. This is what Jesus also meant when He said that to see the Kingdom of God, one must be born again—born of the spirit. From the burning bush, God defined Himself to Moses in the Book of Exodus as 'I Am That I Am,' the word 'that' implies pure spirit or pure consciousness.

"Christ's own life," he continued, "symbolized His message. Through His crucifixion and resurrection, Jesus showed us that we must become free from the original sin of false identification with a body of flesh. We must rid ourselves of the feeling that we are a limited person and regain the awareness of our undivided perfection as pure spirit. The same holds true of the words 'enter the Kingdom of God,' which is not a place up in heaven or anywhere else, but an inner state of awareness."

"An awareness of what?" I asked.

"Not of what, just an awareness of being. In other words, the awareness that we are nothing but pure being or pure consciousness. 'The Kingdom of God cometh not with observation,' meaning it is not a place outside of you. 'Neither shall they say, Lo here! or, lo there! for, behold, the Kingdom of God is within you,'" he quoted from the Gospel of Luke.

"When Christ says, 'behold,' He is asking us to turn our attention within and merge once again with our innate God consciousness. And when Christ said in the Gospel of John, 'I am the way and the truth and the life, no one comes to the Father except through me,' he was not referring to his physical body or personality. He was referring to His innate consciousness, which was one with God.

"God said to Moses in Exodus, 'Thus you shall say to the sons of Israel, I Am has sent me to you,' while Jesus said in the Gospel of John, 'Before Abraham was, I Am,' which proves Jesus knew and experienced Himself as the eternal I Am awareness, and not as a person that lived in a particular time and place."

"Does this mean we shouldn't pray to Jesus, to his form?"

"No. We should pray to His form, His image, because it fills our heart with delight. But if our understanding of Jesus is limited to His human body, our communion with Him will be hampered by our ignorance. Through deep contemplation, we should understand Jesus for what He really was—the eternal power behind all of creation. Jesus is and will always be the pure awareness 'I Am,' which pulses in our heart and bears witness to our mind. If we want salvation, all we need to do is turn our attention to the spirit within."

I sat in the small compartment, mesmerized by what I was hearing, but it didn't take long for my mind to wander back to my own mortality.

"Father, there's one more thing."

"Yes, my child?"

"Last time you spoke to me about death. Am I going to die?"

"I just reminded you that everyone must die."

"No, from this disease. Imminently."

"My child, I'm not a fortune teller."

"I'm sorry," I said, feeling stupid for asking.

I was about to leave when a thought flashed through my mind.

"I've been coming here all this time, but I can't say that I even know your name. We haven't even met face-to-face."

The priest chuckled. "Then wait for me outside."

I stepped out of the penitent's compartment and looked around the empty church. Everything was quiet and peaceful. For about a minute I stood with bated breath, my hands clasped together like a schoolgirl waiting to be called into the principal's office. Then the center door clicked open. When he emerged into the light, he wasn't anything close to what I had imagined. I expected a heavyset man with squinting eyes and a bulbous nose. Instead the priest was tall, at least six foot, with a square jaw and perfectly straight black hair. His green-gray eyes beamed like stars against his pale skin, and they drew in all my attention without effort. Although I was embarrassed to admit it, he was more handsome than I had envisioned. I smiled awkwardly, feeling that the wisdom of his words was oddly out of place with his appearance. As he stepped closer, the lines around his eyes came into view, revealing that he was probably in his mid-forties.

He stood before me, his lips opening up to a smile.

"I'm Father Manann," he said, extending his hand.

When I shook it, it was cold to the touch.

"Laura McDermott," I replied.

For a moment, we looked at each other in silence.

"Well, I can finally put a face to the voice," I said nervously.

He nodded and observed me with a soft but focused gaze.

"I'm glad to finally meet you," he said, breaking the hold that had come over me.

"Me, too," I replied, not knowing what else to say.

I stared at him for another few seconds, almost shamelessly, unable to tear my eyes away from him. And it had nothing to do with his appearance. There was something operating at a much deeper level, an aura or energy that kept my eyes glued to his, something on the verge of hypnotic.

When he saw me standing there like a fool, he again spoke. "My child, I know you are scared, feeling as if you are struggling through this on your own, but let me assure you that the Lord is with you at all times. You are never alone, not for a second."

"Thank you," I said.

He smiled again, his eyes brimming with compassion. After a quick nod, he turned around and disappeared into the confessional.

~

I sat in my car for some time, unable to turn the key. The mysterious blanket of peace I had felt when I first stumbled upon the church enveloped me once again, but now its presence loomed stronger than ever, infusing me with a sense of absolute calm and serenity. But unlike before, I was certain of its origin. I knew intuitively this unexpected peace traced straight back to the priest. He was its source, and it had followed me all the way back to the car like the lingering fragrance of a sweet perfume.

Who is this man? I asked myself, though, in reality, I felt no desire to search for an answer. Instead, I closed my eyes and yielded to the irresistible pull of the moment.

THE LANCET

*W*hen I awoke from the operation to remove my lymph nodes, Anthony, Claire, Jill, and my mother were all standing around my bed. Seeing them together in the same room brought an immediate smile to my lips.

I turned my head but felt a tug from the drainage tube stapled to my lower neck. A thick foam wedge elevated my leg, and I noticed a second tube protruded from under my knee. Now that most of the lymph nodes in those areas were gone, I was at risk of developing a condition called lymphedema, a chronic swelling caused by a buildup of excess fluids that the nodes normally handle. To reduce the risk, the doctors fitted me with compression stockings and prescribed medication which caused me the indignity of having to pee excessively.

Dr. Cardoso, my lead surgeon, dropped by my bed a few hours later.

"Everything is clear and looking good," he said in his heavy Brazilian accent.

～

I was discharged a week later without any complications except for some minor swelling and tingling at the back of my knee. Because the drainage tubes were still in place, I was ordered to stay in bed as much as possible to guard against creeping lymphedema. That suited me just fine since the trips to and from the bathroom were hard enough.

On the bright side, my mother had moved into my extra bedroom and had taken to pampering me around the clock, which I was thoroughly enjoying. I couldn't remember the last time I had eaten a clay-baked olive chicken like the one that appeared one night on my bedside tray, and I realized how much better off I would have been if my mother had been there during my chemotherapy.

Anthony again moved the TV into my bedroom to help me through the day, though I rarely switched it on. Instead, I spent most of my time on my laptop trying to advance the paper, but without physical access to the trial records, there was only so much I could do.

One afternoon, my mother came across an old cardboard box tucked away in my bedroom closet.

"What's this?" she asked.

"Nothing. Just stuff I keep dragging around."

Without asking, she removed the lid and started digging through the contents.

"Oh, look at this," she said, "your award from the state science fair for your research on Greenland sharks. I remember that. And here's your high school diploma."

There were other odds and ends: old passports, university transcripts, faded pictures from my childhood, and letters my father had sent me while I worked on Governor King's campaign.

Then my mother unearthed a small black-and-white wedding picture of Jeremy and me, standing by the sea. She dusted the frame and stared at it for a moment.

"Shame," she said. "A real shame. You made such a nice couple."

~

Twelve days later, with my wounds healing nicely, I returned to Mass General to have my staples and tubes removed. When I got home, I found the following email from Dr. Connor.

Laura, I'm sorry to drop you a line in this way, but I have been exceptionally busy. First of all, I'm thrilled to hear your surgery went well and I wish you every success with the upcoming TIL treatment. As always, we have our fingers crossed for you. That said, I know I signaled in our last conversation that we could put the paper aside until you recovered. Sadly, after sitting down with the sponsor, I've been forced to reconsider. I've been instructed to move right ahead and submit ASAP. It's simply a question of market pressure given the similar protocols that Gendler-Léman Pharma is developing.

I know this will come as a terrible disappointment to you, but the silver lining is that it will free your mind to focus on your next round of chemotherapy. Moreover, there will always be another trial and another paper for you to author down the road. As you know, I've been through this process many times before and I have no intentions of retiring anytime soon. Given Medalux's demands on me, I've transferred the paper to Michael, effective immediately, in whom I know you have a great deal of confidence. Again, I'm deeply sorry for this unfortunate news, but I trust that I have your understanding. I also apologize for informing you by email. I promise to call in the next few days. We are all rooting for you and hope to see you back soon. Kind regards, Brendan.

I sat for a second, unable to believe what I had just read. I reread it twice to make sure that I wasn't hallucinating. What astonished me was his audacity to suggest my removal from the paper was in my best interests. The suggestion of future opportunities shocked me, given the real possibility that this would be my first and last opportunity to publish in such a prestigious journal. And though I conceded that our sponsor was putting a lot of pressure on him, there was no excuse for telling me by email. At the very least, he should have come by with flowers in hand.

I remained stunned, trying to process what had just happened. I knew Dr. Connor well enough to read between the lines. He had looked at my recurrence and concluded that I wasn't going to make it. Otherwise, despite the pressure from above, he would have done something—anything—to keep me on board.

I called Anthony in a daze, barely containing myself throughout our conversation. He tried to calm me down by telling me that I might have misinterpreted things, and I should call Dr. Connor. But there was absolutely no way I was going to pick up the phone. Instead, I wanted to see how long it would take Dr. Connor to make good on his promise to call me. My suspicions were confirmed when I still hadn't heard from him after a week's time.

On Wednesday, Anthony invited my mother and me over for dinner. As I passed around the coffee and carrot cake, Anthony revealed how pleased he was that Dr. Connor had sidelined me from the paper.

"Why?" I asked.

"Because you can't possibly go through another round of chemo while worrying about a paper. Don't you realize Dr. Connor has a point?"

"No, I don't," I shot back. "The TIL process only takes five weeks. So what am I supposed to do when I get back to work? Start from scratch?"

Anthony shrugged.

"Do you think it's fair, after such a long clinical trial, to lose a golden opportunity because I'm out for a miserable five weeks?"

Anthony turned red in the face and pointed his fork at me. "This is about your life, Laura, not your career. Your life!" he yelled. "What difference does it make if you're out of commission for a month? You should be fighting your cancer with total attention, but you keep acting as if it's just another nuisance to be swept aside.

"Dr. Connor did you a favor," he added. "The one thing out of line was that he didn't bother to come in person to tell you. But knowing you, I don't blame him because—"

"All right, that's enough," my mother jumped in.

"No, it's not," I snapped back, turning to Anthony. "Can't you see I need this? If you haven't figured it out yet, the idea of seeing my name in *The Lancet* is the only damn thing keeping me going."

Anthony put his fork down and wiped his mouth with his napkin.

"*The Lancet, The Lancet*," he repeated, throwing his hands in the air. "Why can't you just live for life's sake? Why do you obsess about being recognized? Are you really that shallow?"

"Please," my mother said. "We didn't come here to be bullied."

A THREAD OF HOPE

*E*ver since I went back on medical leave, my work at the hospital had reduced to a trickle. Only a handful of patients currently in remission remained under my care, and anyone who developed complications was quickly reassigned to another physician.

I obsessed over the TIL treatment over the next three days. Would I be a responder? Would it save me? The TIL cells had been harvested from the tumors removed during my lymph node surgery, and they were being expanded in vitro until they reached around ninety billion cells. The plan was to introduce them back into my body to kill off this melanoma once and for all.

Because there were other patients in line ahead of me, Dr. Yoshimura called the lab every few days to find out when my therapy would begin. Not for another three weeks, was what he had been told.

The constant stress of waiting for the phone to ring was offset, in part, by sightseeing with my mother. I took her to my favorite places in and around Boston: the swan boats at the Public Garden, the John F. Kennedy Library and Museum, the

Freedom Trail, and the town of Newburyport. It was an idyllic time, a gift, in fact, which brought us closer than we had ever been before. But hardly two weeks after we returned from Newburyport, I began to experience a rash of new symptoms which made those days feel like a distant memory.

It started when I woke up in the middle of the night bathed in sweat. I reached beneath my body and noticed my sheets were damp. I got up, took a hot shower, changed the sheets and went back to sleep. The next morning, after breakfast, I felt groggy and crawled back into bed. But I awoke a few hours later with a sharp pain in my stomach. I forced myself to get up and left a message for Dr. Yoshimura.

I found myself sitting in his examination room three hours later, his fingers probing around my neck.

"I can feel some swelling on these lymph nodes," he said. "But just barely."

When he touched my abdomen, pushing down ever so gently, I flinched in pain.

"Let's get you admitted while we figure out what's going on," he said.

The sudden onset of symptoms didn't sit well with my mother, so I spent the next few hours suffering through my stomach pains and downplaying what was happening in the hopes of calming her down.

"It's probably just my medicine doing a number on my stomach," I said.

To get me through the night, they stabilized my pain with oxycodone between wheeling me away for new scans and blood tests.

When Dr. Yoshimura walked into my room the next morning and I saw the look on his face, I knew then and there I was terminally ill.

"Laura, I'm not good at hiding things. I know you're aware the news is not going to be good."

"There's a stomach tumor?" I guessed.

He sat on the edge of my bed, his eyes filled with sadness, and passed me the report. I flipped the pages and saw new tumors detected on my spleen, pancreas, lining of the heart, pelvis, stomach, and spinal cord.

I was dying and we both knew it.

A chill rushed through me followed by silent tears. From my peripheral vision, I saw Dr. Yoshimura trying to pass me a tissue, but I was too numb to react. Then he moved closer and took my hand.

"I'm so sorry," he said. "So very sorry."

"What is it?" said my mother, jumping up from her cot. I gave her the report and when she saw I was sobbing, she also started to cry.

She put her arm around me, and we cried for some time while Dr. Yoshimura massaged my hand. When my breathing settled down, I lifted my red-soaked eyes to his.

Although he was sad, I could sense his fighting spirit.

"Listen. I'm going to make sure you start the TIL treatment as soon as possible, but right now I need to get you into radiation therapy."

"Well, get on with it!" my mother yelled.

Dr. Yoshimura cast her a soft glance. "Ma'am, I know how unbearably difficult this is, but the best way for you to help Laura is by staying calm. I assure you I won't waste a second getting her into treatment."

She nodded and sat back down.

I managed to crack a smile, holding on to that final thread of hope. With so many tumors popping up all at once, surgery was no longer an option. The radiation was not meant as a cure. Its sole purpose was to shrink and hold back the tumors long enough for me to get through the TIL treatment.

The only open question was whether I had any hope of

withstanding the brutal chemo and IL-2 drips that came with the TIL infusion.

"I don't know, but we don't have much of a choice," said Dr. Yoshimura.

After he left the room, I phoned Anthony and Jill to break the news.

THE NINTH VISIT

I spent the next day at Mass General receiving targeted radiation therapy on all my new tumors. For the rest of the week, I stayed in bed recovering from the nausea and sleepiness that came with the treatment.

"Your water bottle is almost empty. Do you want a refill?" asked my mother.

"Thanks. I'm still flushing out the radiation," I said.

By some miracle, I awoke the next morning feeling better, so I put on my coat and headed for the door.

"Where are you going?" my mother asked.

"To church," I replied, leaving her staring at me in disbelief.

When I stepped into the church, I noticed that the green light above the confessional was off. After I dipped my fingers into the holy water, I went about trying to locate someone who could tell me if Father Manann was in, but there was no one to be found.

I made my way past the plaster figures that flanked the

aisles and sat on a pew, letting my eyes rest again on the large statue of Jesus on the cross. As I gazed at him, I realized how much I had come to appreciate the peace and compassion that emanated from that beautiful form. Before I knew it, I felt a tear roll down my cheek. What happened next surprised me even more. I closed my eyes and began to pray.

Lord Jesus, Heavenly Father, if You can hear me, please bless me with Your grace and mercy. I'm suffering, and I'm scared. I'm fighting cancer, and I'm losing.

Yes, I confess that I have sinned. Sinned in my stubborn refusal to believe. Sinned through my pride and ambition. Though You tried many times to reach me after Elaine's death, I failed to heed Your call. And in my own illness I also failed to turn around and face You. But my eyes are now open. Please forgive me. More than anything, I just want to live. Please grant me another chance so I may live and learn how to love You. O, Heart of Compassion, please shower me with Your mercy and forgiveness.

With flowing tears, I searched my pockets for something to wipe them away. When I looked up, I saw an old woman staring at me with kind eyes. I smiled back, unafraid now, and wiped my eyes with a crumpled old tissue I managed to find.

Two days later, my condition worsened. Bedridden, I began to suffer from attacks of diarrhea and weakness, and the right side of my pelvis began to ache. At first, I thought they were the lingering side effects of my radiation, but my intuition told me the tumors were behind it.

I brushed the thought away and tried to remain positive, imagining myself sitting in the airplane on my way down to the hospital in Maryland. But by late evening I was shivering and growing so weak, I could barely lift my arms. My mother, my watchful angel, spent the night wiping the sweat off my brow and making sure I drank lots of water.

Anthony, as usual, made a fuss about coming over to help, but I quickly put a stop to it.

"You have enough on your hands with Claire," I said. "From now on I'm keeping visiting hours just like at the hospital, but shorter. One hour in the evening, nothing more."

By morning I felt well enough to sit up and eat some toast and scrambled eggs. As I sat in my bed, enjoying the sunrise through the window, the inescapable reality dawned on me that I was no longer capable of making it through the TIL treatment. If it moved forward, I would probably succumb to the chemotherapy. I knew full well as a cancer specialist that my body had grown too weak to survive a total bone marrow depletion. And although my mind rallied against the truth, my years of looking at things with a clinical eye cut through my attempts at denial. I was going to die, and there wasn't any science out there that could save me.

The overwhelming force of that realization brought my mind to a standstill. I went blank, so I could no longer hear any sounds or register what my eyes were seeing.

So this is what it feels like to know you are going to die, I thought to myself. Though in truth, I couldn't say that I was feeling much of anything. Then an unexpected calm swept over me, as if to reassure me that everything was unfolding exactly as it was meant to.

My mother's voice cut through my trance. "Laura, are you all right?"

In a half-daze, I managed to get up, shower, and dress. I searched my closet and wrapped myself in a thick woolen coat. I called a cab over my mother's protests, explaining that I needed to get back to the church.

"Then I'll come with you," she offered.

"No. I need to be alone."

When I arrived, I shuffled over to the confessional, my hips and legs a twisted mass of pain. I sat down and slid the chair all the way to the back, allowing my head to rest against the wall. I closed my eyes.

"May our Lord Jesus Christ bless you and bring you into the Kingdom of Heaven."

Hearing that voice again brought a smile to my lips.

"Father," I said, my breathing slow and labored. "I've taken a turn for the worse."

"I'm sorry," he said.

"The tumors. They're everywhere."

"Then let's pray together."

"I prayed to Jesus to heal me, Father, but my prayers have gone unanswered."

"Unanswered does not mean unheard," he said.

"Then why won't He help me?"

"My child, what I'm about to say may not give you any comfort. Maybe the Lord has willed a far greater destiny for you. If only you would trust," he said.

"My fate is sealed," I said, shifting my hips, trying to ease the stabbing pain. "It's only a matter of time," I grunted.

"Then let us pray in silence."

We sat in perfect stillness for a long time. In that silence, all of the words he had spoken to me gathered up to coalesce into a single point of power.

A faint murmur escaped from his lips, breaking the silence. He cleared his throat.

"My child," he said, "I've prayed for you in Jesus' name. If it's true you are close to death's door, then now is the time to rise up and claim the Lord's peace which is your birthright and ever shines within you."

"I'm ready," I mumbled. "Just show me how."

"Let go of all of the burdens that have held you down. Let

go of everything you've ever felt responsible for. Everything,"
he repeated.

"How?"

"Abandon the guilt you've carried with you from the days
of your daughter's death. You were not responsible for her
death. Stop trying to make up for it by working so hard to find
a cure for cancer. You are not responsible for finding a cure.
Stop trying to define yourself through your achievements. Your
soul is already cast in God's image, so there's no need to add
anything to it. Remember what is destined to happen will
happen, however hard you try to avoid it. And what is not
destined to happen will never happen, however much you
strive for it. As I've told you before, surrender your life to God.
Lay all of your burdens at His feet. Why are you holding back
when Jesus already suffered for all of us? Otherwise, you're like
a person on a train who insists on carrying her suitcase on her
head instead of putting it down and letting the carriage bear its
weight."

The priest's words pierced me like an arrow. Everything he
said about my deepest self was true.

"You know me so well."

"My ability to understand you is greater than you realize,"
he said. "You've tormented yourself with guilt for a long time,
fighting God's will instead of accepting it and embracing the
peace that is yours.

"What you need," he continued, "is to forgive yourself. Pray
for forgiveness from the people you've hurt and offer forgiveness to anyone who's hurt you. Offer your deepest forgiveness
and then forgive yourself for all of the needless suffering
you've put yourself through."

"I might find it in me to forgive, but will God forgive me?" I
whispered.

"What is God other than the light of forgiveness? What is

Jesus except the embodiment of forgiveness? If your desire is heartfelt, know that you have already been forgiven."

I started to cry, first quietly, then louder. With those simple words, the priest managed to break through the final layers that covered me, exposing parts of myself that I had long buried. I now understood that the entire thrust of my life, my work, my pride, and everything that came with it, had been nothing but a desperate attempt to compensate for the sadness of Elaine's death.

"Jesus is more than willing to carry your burdens. Right now, at this very moment, set them down at His feet. Love yourself, forgive yourself, and be at peace. Feel grateful for the life you've been given."

I let his words sink in as deeply as I could.

"Tell me, how can I find Jesus?" I asked. "Tell me how I can let go of everything."

"Call out to Him with all your heart. Ask Him, again and again, to receive you into His mercy. Like a child running back to his father, rest your tired forehead in His loving hands. He is waiting for you, and the moment you find Him, you will feel the Lord's peace."

"Thank you," I whispered.

After a moment of silence, I mentioned that I had one final request.

"Yes, my child?"

"It's been a long time, Father, but please accept my confession. Let me be restored to God's grace."

"Carry on," he said.

"Bless me for I have sinned..."

I confessed everything as far back as I could remember, keeping nothing to myself.

"God is most keen to forgive a sin the moment it's been committed," he said. "Do not disparage the Lord's grace by wallowing in guilt and self-loathing, which only leads to more sin. Repent with sincerity and be at peace, remembering your own divinity."

The priest absolved me, and as the sacrament came to an end, I followed him in making the sign of the cross.

"Give thanks to the Lord for He is good," he said.

"And His mercy endures forever," I added.

39

WHEN LEAVES FALL

*T*wo days later Dr. Yoshimura left a message on my cellphone. The lab had finished expanding my TIL cells, and he wanted me to book a flight to Maryland as soon as possible.

When I called him back and told him I had decided not to move forward, he was in complete shock.

"I'll be at your house in an hour," he said.

It took only twenty-five minutes for us to hear a knock on my door. As soon as my mother unlocked the door, Dr. Yoshimura pushed past her and walked straight into my bedroom.

"Laura, I know you feel weak, but we're ready for your TIL treatment. We're ready to launch," he said, trying to infuse excitement into his voice. "You can't quit now."

I shook my head and propped myself up on the pillow.

"I can't," I said.

"Why are you saying that? You know this is our last hope."

"Juro," I said, addressing him by his first name. "Look at me. You know as well as I do, there's no way my body can handle the marrow depletion."

"Laura, the infusion of TIL cells is the only thing we have that can save you. Don't you think it's worth a try?"

"I'll die in the process."

"You don't know that."

"Yes, I do. And I don't want to die in such terrible pain."

Dr. Yoshimura pressed his lips together.

"That's not how I intend to die. I want to die in peace."

"Why are you talking so much about death when there's still hope?" he said.

"There's no hope. I know you feel it's your professional responsibility to follow through to the end. God knows how many times I've done that. It allows you to feel you've done as much as you could, even if it puts me through agonizing pain."

"I'm just trying to save you."

"Yes, as am I."

He stared at me for a second. "Laura, think about this. You need to think as carefully as you can because time is of the essence."

"I know. That's why I want to create the right space so I can face death gracefully. Or at least, try to," I whispered.

Dr. Yoshimura shook his head. "I'll come by tomorrow," he said.

After he left, my mother stood by my bed, almost shaking.

"What's this nonsense about not doing the treatment?"

I tried to explain that I simply wasn't strong enough, but she just started to yell at me. I closed my eyes, waiting for her to calm down. A few minutes later, I asked her to sit next to me and I took her hands into mine. I walked her step by step through the procedure, explaining in detail what the chemo-therapy would do to me and how even with the best pain medication I would still be in terrible agony.

"Either way," I said, "I'll be so weak the odds are they'll have to suspend treatment midway. Or worse, I'll go into cardiac arrest."

But my mother was the most persistent person I knew, and she would have none of it.

"I'm calling Dr. Yoshimura. Even if we have to drag you by your hair to the airport, we'll do that," she said.

"You can't do that."

"Watch me," she threatened.

True to her word, she forced me to hand over his number and called him.

Dr. Yoshimura was back in my apartment a few hours later, trying to convince me to move ahead. My mother had also summoned Anthony for support, though, to my surprise, he didn't say much.

"I'll tell you what," I said. "Set up another CAT scan. If it shows that the radiation shrank the tumors, then I'll agree."

"What's all this about?" my mother asked.

"Mother, I feel sicker than ever. And I know it's because the melanoma is spreading."

Dr. Yoshimura thought about it and nodded. "I'll make it happen today," he said.

In need of fresh air, I asked Anthony to place a chair by my bedroom window. As a gentle breeze caressed my face, I noticed, far down the road, a large oak tree towering over the pavement. A sudden gust of wind shook it violently, and a number of leaves came loose.

Let the leaves fall, I thought to myself.

After the scan, I was admitted to a bed since the pain in my hip made it difficult to travel back and forth to the hospital. Dr. Yoshimura walked into the room about four hours later, looking as somber as ever. My mother and Anthony stared at him, waiting for the verdict.

"The radiation shrank the tumor in the stomach, but there's

substantial growth in the lining of the heart and spine, as well as pelvic bone lesions. Unfortunately, your spine is already showing signs of compression."

What he was trying to say was that unbearable pain would soon develop there as well, and the growth of the melanoma in the lining of my heart explained why I was always so tired and short of breath.

Dr. Yoshimura gazed at me with sadness. By his silence I understood he now agreed with me. My cancer-stricken heart wouldn't allow me to survive the TIL treatment.

My mother, sensing something bad, spoke up. "But she can still do the treatment, right?"

Dr. Yoshimura hesitated for a moment. "I'm sorry, Mrs. McDermott, but Laura is right. It's likely that she would not make it through the treatment."

"But she should at least try!" she snapped back, turning to Anthony for support. "Why are you standing there like a mute? Say something!"

Anthony shook his head. "As terrible as this is, I've watched Laura suffer through five cycles of chemotherapy. Now even he agrees she can't survive it, and they're both cancer physicians."

Anthony's eyes moistened, forcing him to pinch the bridge of his nose to steady himself. He looked up, his eyes swollen with tears.

"I've seen what this chemo does so I'm not going to put pressure on her. If it's true that nothing can be done, then what else can I do but offer my support?" he said, his voice quivering.

As soon as she heard those words, my mother buried her face in her arm to muffle her sobs. Dr. Yoshimura rushed over and hugged her, helping her to a chair.

40

GOD'S JUDGMENT

*I*t took several weeks for my mother to come to terms with the reality that I was dying. And though I don't think she was ever able to accept it, she reached a place where she wasn't fighting it on an hourly basis.

As time passed, my condition deteriorated. My appetite diminished, I felt weak all the time, and the pain in my spine grew to unbearable proportions. To manage it, Anthony drove me to Mass General to receive a final dose of targeted radiation therapy. Beyond that, my sole relief came from a steady rotation of pain medications.

With a prognosis of a few months to live, I turned my attention to putting my affairs in order. I hired a lawyer to draft a will, naming my mother as my beneficiary. Paintings and other objects of sentimental value would go to her, along with a small portfolio of stocks I had cobbled together over the years.

It was sad, to say the least, to find myself in the reverse situation of having to bequeath my belongings to my mother. Just another one of cancer's endless small cruelties.

To Anthony, I gifted the Cartier diamond watch that Jeremy's parents had bought me as a wedding gift.

"Something solid and shiny to remember me by," I said half-jokingly.

"You don't need to give me anything," he said.

As for my accommodations, Dr. Yoshimura helped me to arrange, along with my insurer, for a palliative care room at Mass General's Cancer Center. Instead of having a stream of people coming and going from my apartment, my pain would be easier to manage under the care of an end-of-life support team. Unlike some folks, I had no hang-ups about dying in a hospital room. Hospitals had long since become a second home to me. Spending my last days in my apartment would have also placed a terrible burden on my poor mother.

I sat in my bed the following morning and typed out my resignation letter to Dr. Connor, thanking the Dana-Farber Cancer Center for the privilege of working with them. But when it came time to thank Dr. Connor personally, I felt angry and betrayed. Here I was, dying of cancer, and he hadn't even bothered to send me a concerned email. It was as if he had elbowed me out the moment that he decided I was terminal.

I pushed my feelings aside and forced myself to jot down some diplomatic words before hitting the print button. As I folded the letter, another idea occurred to me.

I got dressed and summoned Anthony to pick me up.

"Where to?" he asked.

"To my office."

With the help of a walking cane, I managed to make it down the hall that led to the pediatric hematology wing. When I reached Dr. Connor's office, I opened the door without knocking. As always, he was hunched over his desk. When he looked up and saw me, an expression of disbelief swam over his face.

"Laura, my goodness, please come in."

He jumped up and ran to the door, taking my elbow as I ambled to the seat. He sank back into his chair after I lowered myself, his eyes unable to conceal his guilt.

"How are you?" he asked, ashamed.

"I've seen better days," I said, knowing that to his eye I must have aged ten years.

"Allow me to apologize for—"

I raised my hand. "No need to smooth things over."

He looked at me and nodded. "I'm sorry. Things got out of control and—"

"Yes, yes, yes. Work, work, work," I said with a wave of my hand.

I sat there on the verge of panting, for even speaking tired me out.

Dr. Connor shaped his hands into a triangle and rested his chin on his fingers. "How much time?" he asked.

"A few months, a few weeks. I don't know."

"Well, I'm so, so sorry," he repeated. "I've behaved poorly. So tell me, how can I make up for it?" he said, rather wryly. "You have every right to be upset at me."

I shook my head. "I'm not looking for anything. I wanted to give this to you in person," I said, handing over my letter of resignation.

He removed it from the envelope and read it, nodding as he went along. Then he gazed at me without uttering a word, as if searching for the right way to say goodbye.

"I want you to know," I said, before he had a chance to speak, "that I forgive you for what you did. I'd like to believe that your intentions weren't bad, just that you have some trouble seeing beyond the tip of your nose."

"Ouch." He grimaced. "Look, I never said I was perfect. But in my defense, did you know I'm giving you credit as a cowriter along with Michael? I wouldn't have it any other way."

"No, I didn't," I replied. "But this is what I'm referring to. Why didn't you send me a simple email?"

Dr. Connor raised his eyebrows and shrugged, putting on an "I'm guilty" look that fell somewhat short of apologetic.

"You never did care for the soul behind the lab coat. All that mattered was your work," I said.

"I guess I screwed up."

I pretended not to hear him. To my surprise, the news that my name would make it into *The Lancet* no longer elicited any feelings in me.

"Tell Michael it's thoughtful of him, but I would prefer it if he took full credit. He wrote it after all."

"Yes, but on the basis of your hard work. So there's no way I'm going to accept that."

"So be it." I sighed. "It doesn't matter anymore."

Dr. Connor looked perplexed. I leaned into my walking cane and pushed myself up, causing him to bend forward to assist me. But I stretched out my hand to stop him.

"I'm fine," I said.

When I reached the door, I turned to face him one last time.

"To have worked here on this particular trial was more than I could have asked for. Thank you for giving me that chance."

"I made the right choice," he said. "You're one of the best doctors I've ever had on my team. I'm not just saying that either."

I made an effort to smile. "Save as many children as you can."

Dr. Connor nodded. "Laura, I'm sorry it has to be this way. There's no justice in this world."

I smiled again. "I trust in God's judgment," I said, before turning around and closing the door behind me.

41

A WELCOME SURPRISE

a week later, Anthony packed and hauled everything back to his house for storage while I settled into my room at the Cancer Center. The space felt large and comfortable. Unlike a typical hospital room, this one was set up to resemble a home. Cream-colored wallpaper covered the walls, along with some lovely oil paintings. There was a dresser, a corner desk, and a few lamps. The windows were large and bright, with a view to the northeast, and it occurred to me that this was a place as fitting as any in which to die.

As I walked down the hall that afternoon, my eyes fell on a magazine lying on a chair. *Happy New Year! How to keep your 2011 resolutions in three easy steps.* I stared at it for a second, realizing that the passage of time had barely registered in my mind. The thought of people out in the world living their normal lives had become foreign to me. Time felt as if it moved at a crawl, the natural flow of life pinned down by death's certain grip. Only the hospital and its adjuncts existed for me: the fluorescent-lit hallways, the smell of the medications, the droning PA system, and the army of doctors and nurses. All of it coalesced into a cast of characters and sounds that turned my life into a waking dream.

That night, after everyone had left and I was alone with a book, I felt Elaine's presence manifest in the room for the second time in my life. I sat up and looked around, even though I knew there was nothing to be seen. And yet, despite my rational mind kicking into full gear, I could not deny Elaine's peaceful but unmistakable energy in the room. It was as if she were welcoming me, letting me know that I was not alone.

"Elaine?" I whispered. "Honey, is that you?"

A few tears rolled down my cheeks and then, as quickly as she had arrived, she was gone. The room went back to feeling empty except for the steady hum of the hallway ice machine in the background.

In the morning, with my laptop resting on my thighs, I began browsing for summer courses. When Anthony dropped by to check on me, I let him know that I had registered Claire for an eight-week workshop at a photography school in Paris, the city of her dreams.

"What do you mean?" he asked.

"It's done. Paid in full. She leaves in early July."

"How much?"

"It doesn't matter. It's the least I can do."

Anthony shook his head. "Whatever it is, I'm paying you back."

"You're not thinking straight," I told him. "What would I do with the money?"

"That's not the point," he said.

"Please don't ruin this for me. I can't wait to see the smile on her face," I said.

Anthony smiled and sat down at the edge of my bed.

"If you're sure about it, then okay. But as much as I wish she could come here to visit you, I don't think Claire can handle seeing you...like this," he said. "This business of dying is more than she can deal with."

I couldn't deny that he was right. "I understand," I said. "But I need her to know that I've had a change of heart. Tell her that following your dreams is the most important thing you can do. Tell her I'm sorry I wasn't more supportive."

Although it sounded cliché, I actually believed what I had just said.

"You bet. And she's going to be over the moon about Paris," he said, kissing me on the forehead.

As the days ebbed away, so did my strength. New, throbbing pain made its presence felt in every corner of my body, and the aching in my tumor-ridden bones had worsened. Dr. Yoshimura switched me from a diet of oxycodone pills to much stronger morphine tablets. To counterbalance the nausea caused by the opioids, I was given an antiemetic along with something to reduce the inflammation in my spine.

The number of drugs in my system meant I had to be checked every few hours, so I was rarely alone. Someone always came by to stare at the vital signs monitor next to my bed or to draw blood. That meant my privacy was a thing of the past, but at least I was still capable of using the toilet and shower unassisted.

As I gazed out of the window one afternoon, lost to my thoughts, I heard a knock on the door. Anthony and my mother stepped into the room and stood by the dresser as if waiting for a third person to walk in. The door swung open, and none other than Jeremy Holt stepped into view holding a clutch of flowers in hand.

I blinked to make sure it was really him. He looked older, the mark of time visible on his face, but he was still as handsome as ever. He sported a slight tan and wore a pin-striped blue suit with a white shirt.

He stood, gazing at me, no doubt adjusting the image in his mind of a young healthy Laura against the grim reality of the person lying before him. I looked away for a second, embarrassed at myself.

"Laura," he said. "Can I come closer?"

I smiled and gestured for him to come and sit on the chair by the side of the bed.

Jeremy smiled and searched the room for something to place the flowers in.

"I'll find a vase," Anthony said, grabbing the flowers from his hand and exiting the room. My mother sensed that she should also leave and followed his lead.

Jeremy sat and clasped his hands together.

"I'm so sorry. I just found out a few days ago."

"Who told you?"

"I received an email from Anthony. He explained who he was and told me your mother had insisted that he contact me."

My mother had always been fond of Jeremy. "I guess it didn't take long to find you," I said, wondering why I had never bothered over the years to Google his name.

Jeremy smiled. "After the email, I called and we spoke. I was devastated when I heard." He paused for a second, unsure of himself. "I hope you're okay that I'm here."

I nodded. To my surprise, I felt my eyes moisten.

"How have you been?" I asked, taking hold of his hand.

It turned out that he had spent a number of years wandering around the far reaches of the globe. After staying in Greece, he'd skipped his way across Europe, Israel, Jordan, and India. He finally landed in Australia, where he lived for almost six years.

It was there, he said, where he met his current wife, Bethany, and it was she who helped him piece himself back together. "I owe her no less than my life," he said.

From politics, he had shifted into banking. After making a name for himself, he was offered a job as Vice President of Risk and Compliance at a bank in Zurich, where he currently resided with his family. He had two kids, Olivia and Alexander, ages six and three.

"I'm so happy for you," I said, fidgeting. "I'm sorry I look like crap," I laughed.

Jeremy shook his head and squeezed my hand. "I just wish I had known about this a long time ago. I would have come sooner."

I gave him a warm look and said, "They tell me I might have another three months, but I know it's more like one. At best."

"You keep fighting," he said.

I gazed at him with soft eyes. "No. I'm past all that now."

Jeremy looked aside and frowned. "I'm sorry for all the misery I put you through. The misery I put us through."

"There's nothing to apologize for. I know you were only trying to save her, and I should have listened. I should have been more open-minded," I said.

Jeremy shrugged, his eyes welling up.

"I should have listened," I repeated.

"We tried our best," he said.

I nodded.

"It was not our fault," he said.

I nodded again, despite the deep sense of loss clawing at my heart.

"You understand it was not our fault," he repeated.

"I know," I whispered.

"I didn't hear you," he said.

"I know," I said loudly.

"Good," he replied, both of us now in tears. "Now, why

won't you fight this?" he asked.

I shook my head. "I'm tired. I'm done with masks or false hopes. Death is near, and I should at least try to make myself ready. There's no point in denying it. The truth is, I've got no fight left in me. I crave peace, nothing but peace, and I'm looking forward to meeting Elaine soon."

That comment caused Jeremy to lift his chin. He leaned in and spoke slowly. "Well then, you tell her when you see her how much I love and miss her and think about her every day. Every day," he emphasized.

I smiled. "I will, though I can tell you that she already knows."

He smiled back at me.

"I've felt her presence, Jeremy. Right here in this room, just a few nights ago. And it wasn't the first time."

He smiled again and squeezed my hand even tighter.

"There are also times," I continued, "when I've felt a deep blanket of peace come over me. And when I open my eyes, the room is bathed in light." I smiled again. "You probably think I've gone crazy, but you're going to be even more surprised by what I'm about to tell you."

"Try me."

I placed my other hand over his.

"I've found faith, Jeremy. I've found faith in God."

But instead of furrowing his brow, which is what I expected of him, he just nodded.

"Can you believe it? Of all people, I've come to have faith in God," I said, grinning.

"That shows there's hope even for the hopeless," he joked.

I was confused. "But you were the biggest atheist of all. You used to poke fun at religious people, remember?"

Jeremy nodded. "Yes, but that was a long time ago. By the time I landed in Israel, I was in such bad shape I seriously thought about ending it all. In Jerusalem, I visited one church after another, first as a tourist, then for the peace and quiet I felt in them. While I was down in Eilat, of all places, I was sitting on a bench overlooking the sea when it hit me out of the blue. I had been wrong about so many things, but especially about God."

I was stunned. "What changed your mind?"

"I don't know. It's not like I had some earth-shattering spiritual moment that brought me to my knees or anything. It was a subtle, yet unmistakable, breakthrough. I just knew, intuitively and without a shred of doubt, that God exists. Period. In fact, it became as obvious to me as the Red Sea stretching before my eyes," he added.

We unclasped our fingers and looked at each other in mutual understanding.

"I guess you have to trust," he said, his voice now serious, "that what's happening is in accordance to God's will."

"I do, but I'm still afraid."

"Keep praying," he said. "Keep telling yourself that you are safe in God's hands."

Jeremy and I spent as much time together as we could. We traded stories and reminisced about Elaine. Then on Wednesday, after a difficult and emotional final goodbye, Jeremy caught his flight back to Zurich.

That night, after the hospital had grown still, I sobbed quietly in my bed, thanking God for all of the blessings He had showered upon Jeremy, for lifting him out of a dark place and allowing my final memories of him to be happy ones. We had separated under such terrible pain, and now we had come full circle. I felt, by God's grace, another weight lift from my shoulders. Deep down I knew Jeremy's visit had been no accident, but a carefully planned step in preparing me for death.

42

HOME AGAIN

*W*hatever life was left in me began to slip away about a month and a half after Jeremy's visit. The melanoma tumors had penetrated deep into my organs, and their growth was no longer a concern. The hospital's only purpose was to help me to die as comfortably as possible.

Although my mind was still lucid, my mounting pain caused Dr. Yoshimura to switch me from morphine tablets to fentanyl patches, a drug one hundred times more potent than morphine. The cancer continued to ravage my body, even as my pain was brought under control, thinning out my arms and legs until I was reduced to a mere shadow of my former self. When I grew too weak to eat, they started feeding me through a tube. And since I was no longer able to walk, they cleaned and bathed me right from my bed.

A week later, my skin began to emit an acrid, unpleasant smell. My cheeks sunk deep into my face, and my lips became drawn. I drifted into long episodes of sleep, while at other times I remained awake for hours on end as if my mind were trying to cling to the body for as long as it could. My mother stayed with me around the clock, while Anthony and Jill took turns to keep me company, practically putting their lives on hold so they could be with me.

One morning, when I was particularly alert, I gathered everyone around the bed and began saying my goodbyes. I told them how much I loved them and how lucky I was to have been able to share my life with them. But instead of appreciating what I was trying to convey, my mother grew distraught. She asked me if she should call for a doctor, and whether I felt I was about to die. I explained that, no, I didn't feel I was at death's door, only that I didn't want to squander the chance to speak my heart while I still could with a clear mind.

"Think of how tragic it must be for those who die unexpectedly, unable to say goodbye, instead of the opportunity I'm being given. This is one of the blessings of dying slowly," I said.

A week later, as I listened to the labored sound of my lungs rising and falling, I had to shield my eyes with my hand because I thought someone had rolled a large light into the room. When Anthony asked what was wrong, I pressed the incline button on my bed until it raised me to a sitting position. Squinting, I was amazed to discover a diffused, vibrating white light filling the entire room. To my immense surprise, Father Manann stepped up to the foot of my bed. He was smiling, with his hands clasped together in front of his waist.

"Father Manann, what a pleasant surprise."

I heard whispering in the background.

"What is it darling?" my mother asked.

As she spoke, Father Manann stood there quietly.

"Mother, Anthony, Jill, this is Father Manann. He's the priest I've been meeting with at the church down the road." The room fell silent for a moment. Then I felt my mother's hand on my forehead.

"Laura, darling, perhaps you should close your eyes for a little while," she said. Then she turned her head and ordered Anthony to go find a nurse.

I was confused for a second, not understanding what was happening.

"My child, there's no need for you to keep your eyes closed," I heard.

When I opened them, I saw that Father Manann had taken a seat at the edge of my bed. I glanced at my mother, who was standing to my left. Then I looked at Jill, who was staring at me from the back of the room. Neither of them appeared to be able to see the priest.

"My child," he said, in his usual soothing voice, "your suffering is almost at an end."

"They can't see you," I said.

"No, they can't."

"But how?" I asked.

Anthony returned with a nurse.

"She's in the grip of some kind of hallucination," my mother voiced across the room.

I did my best to ignore her and focus on the priest.

"Why can't they see you?" I asked again.

"Best to take a step back," the nurse advised my mother, "and let it run its course. These things are not uncommon," she said.

"My child, our Father has sent me to deliver a final message. Your time of clinging to this frame of flesh and blood is drawing to its end. You needn't struggle any longer, but rejoice in the knowledge that the infinite bliss of heaven awaits you."

I shook my head, still confused as to why no one else could see or hear him.

"What's happening?" I asked. "Am I hallucinating?"

"Yes," I heard the nurse's voice. "But it'll pass. Just close your eyes and breathe."

I didn't listen. "Father, how did you find me? Why are you here?"

The priest gazed at me, his eyes overflowing with compassion, his noble face calm and poised. "I am simply a limb from God's tree, doing as I have always done, carrying out the role I have been ordained to carry out since the dawn of time," he said.

"I don't understand," I said.

"I am here to take you to the Lord. A boatman, if you will, but not the type who ferries you across earthly waters. My reach is beyond the spheres, beyond all waters, into the radiant Light itself."

"Death!" I exclaimed. "You're saying you are death!" As soon as I uttered those words, I felt a shudder in the depths of my heart.

"What's happening?" my mother shrieked. "Do you feel you're dying? Nurse! Please call a doctor!"

The priest nodded, his green-gray eyes glittering brighter than ever. "There's no need to be frightened, for I am one with the Lord. I am simply an agent of His divine will who can do nothing contrary to His design. My only function is to release souls from their bodily prisons at the exact time that He has commanded."

I looked at him, unable to speak, unable to think.

"But how?" I repeated. "All our meetings at the church, in the middle of the day..."

"They were real," he said. "As real as you sitting here in this bed. Is there anything beyond God's power to accomplish?"

I shook my head.

"Matter is nothing but light in God's hands, to be fashioned into any place, shape, or circumstance.

"Your time is near," he continued. "Turn your attention to the indwelling Lord, our only source of fulfillment. Let your heart melt in divine love. Absorb your mind in Christ, and all will be well. You needn't do anything more."

I listened to his words, still questioning whether I had fallen into some kind of trance. As I watched, the expanse of light grew brighter and brighter, first absorbing the priest into itself, followed by the entire room until nothing except the pulsating white light remained.

When I woke up, Dr. Yoshimura was standing next me.

"How are you feeling, Laura?" he asked.

I blinked a few times. "Fine," I managed to say.

"It looks like you suffered a hallucinatory episode," he said. "Most likely from too much fentanyl. I've changed your patch to a lower one, but it'll take some time until the current load works its way through your system."

I nodded silently.

"Do you remember anything?"

In fact, I did. I remembered everything the priest said down to the last word.

Dr. Yoshimura smiled and rested his hand on my shoulder. "If this lower dosage doesn't manage your pain, call me right away."

I closed my eyes, too tired to speak, and pressed the button that lowered the bed.

～

As the hours rolled by, I thought of what the priest had said, that he was simply an agent of God's will, a helper. Maybe that's why death is commonly referred to as the Angel of Death. I remembered the deep peace I experienced each time I came in contact with him, and the image of death as an angel felt oddly appropriate. Perhaps in my fear of death, I had misunderstood him. Death was not a dark specter or a hooded skeleton wielding an ominous sickle, but a force sent by God Himself to release us from our earthly shackles. Death was not a villain or a thief, but a friend who would carry me safely to the other side.

The implication of what I was thinking caused me to shudder. Was it possible that I had been sitting with an otherworldly presence all this time? And in the broad light of day?

I started to breathe rapidly, my mind spinning out of control. But as soon as I closed my eyes, I was seized by a calmness that slowly dissolved my fear, and I smiled at the thought that, even at this late stage, the priest was reaching out to me. Despite my relief, a small part of me remained convinced that I had hallucinated the entire thing.

"Anthony," I whispered, gesturing for him to come over.

"Yes, Laura?"

I struggled to clear my throat. My mouth was so dry that it took a few tries before I was able to speak.

"I need ... a favor," I said weakly.

"What can I do? What do you need?"

"There's a church on Garden Street. Just down the road. Saint John of the Cross," I whispered.

"A church?"

"You don't know this, but I've been going there for a while. There's a priest. Father Manann. I need you to speak to him."

Anthony looked perplexed. He was probably trying to understand how a scientist like me had anything to do with a church.

"What's the name again?"

"Manann," I repeated slowly.

"Let me jot it down," he said, pulling his cellphone out of his pocket. "What does he look like?" he asked.

"Black hair, tall, chiseled face. Late forties," I said. "Tell him my name. Tell him I'm dying, and I want him to visit me." I stopped to catch my breath. "Tell him to hurry."

"I'm going right now," he said.

∾

When I woke up, Anthony was sitting in his chair watching a

Red Sox game. He noticed me stir and came up to the bed. A nurse was adjusting the flow of oxygen through the cannula fitted to my nostrils. Once she left, he spoke.

"How's your pain?"

I nodded, indicating that it was still within acceptable levels, although I was finding it harder and harder to draw a decent breath.

Anthony pulled his chair up to the bed and sat next to me.

"Laura," he began, "I found the church. Halfway down Garden Street just like you said. The thing is, I couldn't find anyone. I waited around until I ran into a priest. But when I asked if he was Father Manann, he just gave me this blank stare.

"He wondered if I had come to the right church because he didn't know anyone by that name."

That comment caused me to open my eyes. "What did he look like?" I managed to ask.

"Oh, he didn't fit your description. The man must have been in his sixties with a head of white hair."

Anthony continued, "I asked him if he was sure he didn't know of a Father Manann. I conveyed your description, but the priest, Father Claybrook, said he was the only one at the church. He mentioned a deacon and a few others who helped him, but that was it."

I looked at Anthony in silence.

"I insisted, don't worry. I asked if the deacon fit your description, or if an outside priest ever came to the church, but he shook his head. He said the deacon was a married fellow of Korean descent.

"Are you sure your priest was a priest?"

I nodded.

"I'm sorry that I couldn't find him."

I closed my eyes and tried to make sense of what was happening. I racked my brain trying to come up with a rational explanation. Had my priest been an imposter who had slipped unseen into the confessional? That was unlikely, given that he had been there every time I showed up. And what of the river of tranquility that swept over me each time I came into his presence? If there was no such priest at the church, it only added to my certainty that I had not imagined his appearance in my room.

I tried to calm my mind by telling myself that it was not a force of evil that had visited me, but a messenger of God, although the idea that death could assume a human form frightened me. I thought back to my visits with the priest and how uplifting they had been until my fear began to give way to an overwhelming sense of wonder. The Lord's guiding presence in this world was more apparent than I could have ever imagined, but, like most people, I simply lacked the eyes to see Him.

∾

As the hours slipped into days, I sank further and further into the opioid fog that had laid claim to my body. Most of my awareness had been reduced to listening to the sound of my shallow breathing and to the whispered conversations around my bed. Sometimes, when spoken to, I could only hear a string of sounds devoid of any meaning, and I was vaguely conscious of the doctors and nurses who tended to me. The world as I knew it was falling away. My greatest hope was to lie quietly, thumbing the pain pump now and then, waiting for death to release me.

Then, in the small hours of the night, I felt my numbness lift, and I found myself in a state of extreme alertness, as if all of the cancer had left my body. I propped myself up against my pillows with barely an effort and saw both my mother and Anthony fast asleep through the darkness, she in her cot and he sprawled over a chair. I cast them a loving glance, knowing that I would not see them again. As I watched, I began to feel light, as if my body's density was being siphoned away. The room pulsed and scintillated with tiny specks of light until, just as before, it was fully enveloped by a soft white glow.

The priest appeared before me and sat down on my bed. He looked ethereal, his lustrous eyes burned brightly, while a gentle smile played upon his lips. He gazed at me for a long time. As serene and profound as he appeared, another tinge of fear passed through me.

"Don't be afraid," he said, his voice calm and reassuring, reaching for my right hand.

As soon as his fingers touched mine, wave upon wave of joy rippled through my body, filling me with a divine ecstasy that made me want to remain in that state forever.

"Now close your eyes and pray to Lord Jesus. Invoke His presence in your heart."

I closed my eyes and began to pray, and, as I did, I started to feel each breath growing longer and slower. The familiar mantle of peace rose up within me once again, though now many times stronger than before. Any traces of fear or resistance left in me evaporated like fog beneath the midday sun. My body began to tingle, and I intuitively knew that the white light surrounding me also pulsated within me as well. My breath continued to grow fine and subtle until it became more life energy than breath. It reached the point where I could no longer feel my lungs playing any part in its ebb and flow. In the background, I could hear the sound of the heart rate monitor flatlining, followed by a flurry of activity around me. Nurses and doctors circled my bed, but I felt entirely removed from the situation as if it were happening to somebody else. The bliss within me intensified until a loud rushing sound reverberated within my head, not unlike the roar of a waterfall. Then an indescribable thrill passed through me and, in an instant, I lost all awareness of my body. I had become a rushing stream of blissful energy, an ecstatic awareness existing within an endless field of shimmering white light. It was in that glorious state that the majestic form of our Lord and Savior, Jesus of Nazareth, manifested before me.

He stood beyond the reach of time, a Presence so vast it felt as if my entire life had been reduced to a grain of sand. His eyes overflowed with love and compassion, and all traces of suffering disappeared. I can't even say I felt peace, for I had become peace. And though I could still remember all the joys and sorrows of my life, they now felt utterly inconsequential, like the dance of tiny ripples on the surface of an immense ocean. Everything was perfect and had always been perfect. I had always been whole.

With a gentle smile, the Lord extended his right hand. "You are home again."

ABOUT THE AUTHOR

Andres Pelenur was born in Argentina and moved to Canada when he was fifteen years old. His love of spiritual knowledge led him to travel extensively throughout India and to go deep into the practice of meditation. Although he misses living next to a South American beach, the cold Canadian winters forced him to curl up on his sofa and devour countless books. When not studying spiritual texts, Andres spends as much time as possible playing with his six-year-old son and traveling to new places.

Printed in Great Britain
by Amazon

47215732R00125